Nadia whirled faster as the music built toward a climax. Her eyes were closed and her arms reached upward into the darkness. The glow of the fire gleamed off the brilliant colors woven into her skirt, and her hair radiated with the dancing flames.

Nothing in his life had prepared Owen for the vision of Nadia dancing. She was primitive and wild—her passion, need, and desire calling to her imaginary lover. Calling to him.

In a final frenzy the music and Nadia came to a sudden stop. She crossed the grass and stood before him. "I danced for you, Owen. Do you know what it means when a woman dances for a special man?"

Owen pulled her with him away from the light of the campfire. "Does it mean you are attracted to me?" he asked.

"It means I want you," she said, pressing her palms against his chest. "I need you, Owen, more than my next breath." She paused, then whispered "I need you more than my music. . . ."

WHAT ARE *LOVESWEPT* ROMANCES?

They are stories of true romance and touching emotion. We believe those two very important ingredients are constants in our highly sensual and very believable stories in the LOVESWEPT line. Our goal is to give you, the reader, stories of consistently high quality that may sometimes make you laugh, sometimes make you cry, but are always fresh and creative and contain many delightful surprises within their pages.

Most romance fans read an enormous number of books. Those they truly love, they keep. Others may be traded with friends and soon forgotten. We hope that each LOVESWEPT romance will be a treasure—a "keeper." We will always try to publish

LOVE STORIES YOU'LL NEVER FORGET
BY AUTHORS YOU'LL ALWAYS REMEMBER

The Editors

Loveswept ® 674

MY SPECIAL ANGEL

MARCIA EVANICK

BANTAM BOOKS
NEW YORK · TORONTO · LONDON · SYDNEY · AUCKLAND

MY SPECIAL ANGEL

A Bantam Book / March 1994

If you would be interested in receiving protective vinyl covers for your
Loveswept books, please write to this address for information:

Loveswept
Bantam Books
P.O. Box 985
Hicksville, NY 11802

ISBN 0-553-44329-1

Published simultaneously in the United States and Canada

Bantam Books are published by Bantam Books, a division of Bantam Doubleday Dell Publishing Group, Inc. Its trademark, consisting of the words
"Bantam Books" and the portrayal of a rooster, is Registered in U.S. Patent
and Trademark Office and in other countries. Marca Registrada. Bantam
Books, 1540 Broadway, New York, New York 10036.

PRINTED IN THE UNITED STATES OF AMERICA

OPM   0 9 8 7 6 5 4 3 2 1

To Gail and Joan,
Thanks for never being more
than a phone call away.

ONE

Owen J. Prescott felt the noose tighten around his neck and yelled, "Are you people out of your minds? Stop it!" The rough rope tying his hands together dug deeper into his wrists.

His feet slid on the hood of the dented station wagon, and he hurriedly regained his balance. He couldn't believe it: His life at the grand old age of thirty-three was about to be ended by a group of ranting Gypsies waving their arms and shouting in some language he didn't understand.

The burly man who had placed the noose over Owen's head jumped from the car, leaving him standing alone. Owen wasn't positive, but they seemed to be yelling at each other now and not at him. He hoped that was a good sign. He was extremely partial to his fifteen-and-a-half-inch neck.

Of all the ways to die, this was definitely not his first choice. He would prefer a scenario that included black satin sheets, lush, creamy thighs, long blond hair, and a Swedish accent. He wanted his smile to be so wide that old Harvey down at the local funeral parlor would have to work overtime to remove it.

Owen glanced around and noticed that the group of men seemed to have forgotten about him standing on the hood of the car with a noose around his neck. He wasn't likely ever to forget; he was planning on telling the sheriff about it as soon as he could figure a way off the Kandratavich ranch. By nightfall either he would be swinging from the end of this rope or the entire Kandratavich family would be looking at the world from behind iron bars. Crows Head, North Carolina, was well known for its rolling foothills, spectacular beauty, and warm hospitality, but this was pushing it too far.

The shouting men were busily gesturing to an approaching group of women and children when the sound of flying horse's hooves caught everyone's attention. The women crossed themselves and hurried forward; the children ran to keep up with their mothers and buried themselves deeper in their colorful skirts. The men slapped their battered hats against their thighs and appeared to be cursing.

Thunder seemed to shake the ground as a huge black stallion quickly ate up the distance and was pulled to a death-defying stop mere inches away from the group and the car. Owen had an impression of smoke billowing from the beast's nostrils as it tossed its mighty head and stomped the ground. He instinctively took a step backward and felt the rope dig deeper into his neck. His gaze slid from the animal to the woman riding him bareback, and his heart seemed to stop. She was breathtakingly beautiful and looked as wild as the mountain laurels that graced the Great Smoky Mountains. Her eyes were dark and just the right size to drown in. Her hair was a curtain of near-black silk, and her pouting mouth was ripe as wild strawberries. Her colorful skirt was yanked around the top of her thighs, giving him a mouth-watering view of small feet sporting blood-red toenail polish and legs that ended somewhere in heaven. Owen felt his heart resume its pounding, somewhere in the middle of his throat. To hell with the blond hair and Swedish accent—this deathbed angel could have him without a struggle.

Nadia Kandratavich pulled her horse to a halt and forced herself to smile pleasantly at her father and uncles. She had seen what was going on from the second story of her house and had set off before anyone could be hurt. Nadia's smile faded when she noticed the discoloration and swelling under her father's right eye. "What's going on, Papa?"

Milosh scowled at the amount of bare leg she was showing in front of the stranger. She sighed and adjusted her skirt, much to the condemned man's disappointment. Milosh nodded his head and started to speak.

"English, Papa, you are now in America," Nadia said, interrupting him.

"This *gadjo* deserves to dance upon the wind."

"What's a *gadjo*?" demanded Owen. He had no idea what it was, but he'd deny he was one with his dying breath.

Nadia looked at the man standing on the hood of her uncle Zanko's car for the first time. Despite the noose around his neck he looked confident, proud . . . and gorgeous. His jaw was tilted at a defiant angle, and fire burned in the depths of his eyes. "It means a person who is not of Gypsy blood."

Owen frowned but kept his defiant stance. He directed his gaze to the lovely woman sitting bareback on the monstrous black beast of a horse. This petite, dark-eyed beauty who seemed to vibrate with life and understanding was the only one who appeared to be listening to him. She also appeared to have some control over the situation. "They are going to hang me because I'm not a Gypsy?"

Nadia smiled. "They were not going to hang you."

He was momentarily thrown off-balance by the brilliance of her smile. It held confidence, a touch of sadness, beauty, and hinted at secrets. He was grateful for the confidence, appreciative of the beauty, and intrigued by the sadness, but above all he yearned to discover her secrets. Returning her smile, he turned his body slightly so she could see that his hands were tied. He glanced up once, following the thick rope from his neck to a sturdy branch of the oak tree overhead. "If they aren't going to hang me, why am I about to be treated like a piñata?"

"Piñata?" questioned Nadia.

"A papier-mâché object that is hung from a tree or another high place." He saw her frown and tried to describe it further. "When you break it open, candy comes pouring out." He bit back a smile as four dark-eyed children peered out from behind their mother's skirts. They had obviously understood the word *candy*. "If you can convince your father and his friends to untie me, I promise to send you the biggest piñata I can find."

Nadia laughed at the look of delight spreading across the youngsters' faces. She sadly shook her head at the handsome man standing on top of Uncle Zanko's newly purchased automobile. "I'm afraid I can't accept your offer."

"Why not?" demanded Owen. He knew a piñata had been a lousy bribe, but he had been exploiting the group's curiosity. What else would an uncivilized group of Gypsies want in exchange for canceling this one-man necktie party?

"Because it would be cheating."

"Cheating who?"

"You." Nadia glanced down at her father, three uncles, and two of her four brothers. "They weren't going to hang you. For some reason they wanted to put a scare into you. When I rode up, they were arguing among themselves if you looked scared enough yet." She smiled brilliantly. "You didn't."

Milosh, Nadia's father, crossed his arms and glared at his daughter. "You know not what he did."

"What did he do that was so offensive, Papa?"

"He called your aunt Celka and Sasha swindlers and cheats." Milosh pushed out his chest as his brothers, Rupa, Zanko, and Yurik, joined him in his stubborn stance. "The Duke would have shot him, but since you won't allow us any guns, we decided to string him up."

"Ellington wouldn't have shot a soul," cried Owen.

Nadia chuckled softly. Someone was obviously a music buff, or he had absolutely no knowledge of cowboy movies. "My father was referring to John Wayne, not Duke Ellington, Mr . . . ?"

"Prescott." He politely nodded his head. "Owen J. Prescott."

"Prescott?" Nadia worried her lower lip between her teeth. "As in Prescott Realty, Prescott Hardware, Prescott Construction, and Prescott Feed Mill?"

Owen clicked the heels of his shoes together and bowed as far as the rope would allow. "At your service, ma'am." He smiled rakishly. "And with whom do I have the privilege of conversing on this fine summer's day?"

She paled to a deadly shade of white and whispered, "Nadia Kandratavich." She turned to the group of men and, breaking her own rule, started to wave her arms and shout directions in a foreign language.

Within seconds Owen found himself breathing easier, as the noose was pulled back over his head and his hands were quickly untied. He refused the helping hand proffered by the same burly man who had set him on the car in the first place. With a smooth jump Owen landed on the ground and started to brush the dirt from his once immaculately pressed pants. "I know you and your family are all relatively new to Crow's Head, but we have a tradition here." He glanced up at Nadia and straightened the collar of his white short-sleeved shirt. "It's called hospitality."

She lost the remaining color in her cheeks. "Mr. Prescott . . ."

"Nadia." He liked the sound of her name as it rolled over his tongue. It tasted foreign and exotic, just as she would. "My name is Owen."

There was no way she was calling him by his first name. The town of Crow's Head should have been named Prescott, Prescottville, or at least Prescott Junction. General Jeremiah Prescott, of the Confederate Army had his own bronze statue decorating the square in the middle of the town, complete with a fierce rearing horse and half an acre of blooming flowers surrounding him. Every other building in town boasted the name Prescott, including the name of the mortgage company that held the deed on this ranch. Owen J. Prescott could wipe her out with one stroke of his pen. "Mr. Prescott . . ."

"Owen." He flashed her a brilliant smile.

Nadia swallowed hard and muttered, "Owen, then." She glanced at her two aunts. "What did Celka and Sasha do?" She silently added, *this time*.

Owen looked at the group of Gypsies and tried to pick out Celka and Sasha by their guilt. He couldn't. Of the four older women standing there, none looked guilty or ashamed. All their weather-beaten faces were tilted up at a proud and stubborn angle. "They sold my aunt Verna a case of bottled water and claimed it was from the Fountain of Youth."

Nadia muttered an explicit curse in Russian and then quickly prayed to a saint for forgiveness. Her family was driving her crazy. Didn't they realize how much she had sacrificed to get them all out of war-torn Europe and into the United States? All she had asked in return was for them to obey the laws, learn English, and stay out of trouble. Obviously even that was too much to ask. "Celka, Sasha, where is his aunt's money?"

A woman who appeared to be in her early forties stepped forward. "Half is in our pockets, and the rest is in our bellies," said Sasha.

"How much did you spend on food?"

"Fifty-eight American dollars," answered Celka.

The horse shifted nervously as Nadia's fingers tightened involuntarily on the reins. Her once-plump nest egg was already down to the size of a golf ball and growing smaller every day. She loosened her grip on the reins and gave her mount a gentle pat. "Easy, boy." The horse calmed immediately. "Give Mr. Prescott what money you have left and an apology. I'll repay the rest, and hopefully he won't press charges against you two." She glared at her remaining family. "I can't say the same for the rest of you. What you did to Mr. Prescott was wrong. I know that you weren't really going to hang him, but what if he had had a weak heart and had died from the fright?" She made eye contact with all the men standing there. "All of you would have been sent to prison for murder." She was somewhat relieved to see their sorrowful expressions. "Before you do something so stupid again, think about spending the rest of your lives behind bars, never to dance under the skies, to sleep under the stars, or hold a loved one close."

She looked down at Owen. "I can reimburse your aunt and offer my apologies on my family's behalf. As for your welcome to the Kandratavich Ranch, I can only assure you that the next time you come to call, you will be received with open arms and the gracious hospitality of my family." She glared at her family and dared anyone to disagree with her. Hopefully Owen wouldn't press charges—she doubted if she had enough available cash to bail them all out. The only thing that could break a Gypsy's soul was to take away his freedom.

Owen stared at Nadia for a full minute before slightly nodding his head. He didn't want this fiery angel's apologies. She hadn't done a thing wrong. When Celka and Sasha stepped forward and slowly handed him the few coins and crumpled bills, he felt like a thief. He glanced at the wide-eyed stare of the children and remembered that Sasha had said that half the money had already gone for food. Were they so desperate for food that they would try to swindle his seventy-two-year-old aunt out of 120 bucks?

Nadia noticed his hesitation and sighed. Mr. Born-with-a-Silver-Spoon-in-His-Mouth Prescott was about to become charitable. "Take the money, Owen. It's rightfully your aunt's."

Owen jammed the money into his pants pocket. Aunt Verna could have bought an entire reservoir of mythical Fountain of Youth water and still not have missed the money. While the Prescott bank accounts were overflowing with zeros, the Prescotts themselves were down to the last two, Aunt Verna and himself. He tended to be a tad overprotective of his only living relative.

He mumbled a soft "Thank you" to Celka and Sasha and wondered how in hell the tables had gotten turned without his even realizing it. One minute he was ready to testify in court against the entire Kandratavich clan, and the next instant he was thanking them. He glanced up at Nadia. "Maybe we could—"

"There's no maybe about it, Owen. Please return the money to your aunt with our apologies." She gracefully slid off the horse and landed softly next to Owen.

He nearly burst a blood vessel as he watched her slide off the back of the black beast of a horse. The flowing kaleidoscope of colors on her cotton skirt had bunched up around midthigh, offering him a view that would have surely sent a priest into confession. Only one word could describe Nadia's tan, satiny legs: heavenly. They surely had to lead the way to the Pearly Gates.

"If you come with me to my house, I will get you the rest of the money." Nadia nodded her head in the direction she had come.

Owen saw a small white house and a huge weather-beaten barn in the distance. "It's not necessary." He didn't want her money, but he was curious about her. He quickly glanced at her left hand. The third finger was bare, but she wore elaborately carved gold rings on two of the others. Her right hand boasted three more rings. She had no husband. Anyone who wore that many rings would surely wear a wedding band.

"I must repay your aunt. It's a matter of family pride." She had noticed him looking at her hands and quickly hid them in the folds of her skirt. Vanity was such a distasteful quality, but she couldn't help it. She felt her hands were her worst feature. They were callused from playing the guitar constantly, and the nails were trimmed so close to the skin that hardly any white showed. Her livelihood, and that of her family, depended on her fingers. She turned to the children. "Who would like a ride up to the house?"

Four urchins disengaged themselves from their mothers' skirts and came running forward. Nadia laughed and swung a boy of about six up onto the horse's back. Owen was entranced by the musical sultriness of her laughter and the love that was illuminated across her face. When she placed all four children onto the stallion's back, she turned and started to lead the horse across the field.

Owen fell in step beside her and marveled at her size. When she had been sitting on top of the stallion, she appeared a lot taller. If Nadia was pushing five foot two, the extra inch was due to her thick wavy hair. His fingers itched to thread their way into the dense darkness and see if it was as soft as it appeared. Dangerous thoughts for a man who five minutes ago was about to have his neck stretched by her family. He glanced behind them and grinned up at the children. Every one of them seemed fearless—both of the beast and of sitting so far up off the ground. Owen returned his attention to the beautiful woman walking beside him. "Does your horse have a name?"

"Of course." The foreign accent punctuating her words wasn't nearly as strong as the rest of her family's. "Don't all American pets have names?"

"Yes, but so far you haven't called him by his. I've been listening."

He glanced at the powerful black stallion. "I bet everything that's in my wallet that his name isn't Buttercup."

Nadia chuckled and dug a cube of sugar out of her skirt pocket, then lovingly held out her hand for the horse. "Not even close."

"I would have gone with a name like Satan or Lucifer."

"Now you're getting warm." She gently rubbed the stallion's nose and softly whispered something in a foreign language. "I named him after something every American fears."

"'Nuclear War'? 'The Dentist'?" He loved the sweet, musical ring of her laughter as it drifted across the field. He continued to tease her: "What about 'Mother-in-Law'?"

Nadia caught her breath. "No, his name is IRS."

Owen stopped in his tracks and stared at the stallion, who at the sound of his name gently nudged the back of Nadia's neck. "Why did you name him after the Internal Revenue Service?"

"He was born on April fifteenth." She held out another sugar cube as they crossed a dirt road in front of the barn and a small fenced-in corral.

He glanced at the barn and shuddered. The entire building was leaning dangerously to the right. Nadia lifted down the children and chuckled as they scampered away in a flash of dark eyes and giggles. Opening the corral gate, he watched as she removed the bridle and gave IRS a gentle pat on his rump. The stallion tossed his head, glared at Owen, and trotted into the corral. Owen latched the gate. "I don't think your horse likes me."

"He's miffed because you didn't give him a treat. He's used to having everyone pass him a goody. IRS is just a big old spoiled baby." She laid the bridle across the crooked, splintered fence and absently picked at a hunk of peeling white paint. One day she hoped to be able to afford to fix up IRS's home and to fill every acre of the Kandratavich Ranch with his progeny. He was the keystone of her dream. IRS represented everything she had been sacrificing for these past years. He was 'the Kandratavich Ranch,' a permanent home for her family at last. Her wandering days were over. She was born in Hungary; by the time she was a month old, she was living in Russia; and by her third birthday she was in what was then Yugoslavia. She was fluent in six languages by the time she was eight and had seen two thirds of Europe by her sixteenth birthday. She would be elated if she never had to step a foot off the Kandratavich Ranch.

"Nadia?"

She jerked back to the present. "Oh, I'm sorry. Did you say something?"

The secrets had reentered her eyes. "Where did you go?"

A faint tinge of pink darkened her cheeks. "I was sweeping the cobwebs." She turned and started to walk toward the house.

He fell in step with her. "Sweeping cobwebs?"

"Isn't that what you call it?"

"Oh." He chuckled softly. "You mean, shaking the cobwebs."

"Same thing." She stepped up onto the porch and opened the screen door. "Sweep or shake cobwebs, and dust will still fly everywhere." She held the door for Owen. "Come in for a moment. I will be right down."

Owen stepped over the threshold and softly shut the screen door behind him. Nadia had already disappeared out of the spacious kitchen. He frowned as he glanced around the room. The counters were empty. No toaster, microwave, or even a dirty coffee cup. The walls had at one time been painted a bright yellow, but over the years they had faded into a dull-looking cream color with only the outlines of pictures or other items revealing their original color. In the spacious area where a table for eight could easily have fit, sat a small table and two wobbly-looking chairs. But Nadia had added a touch of color by covering it with a vibrant hand-painted silk scarf.

He slowly walked out of the kitchen and into the living room. His frown grew deeper. Only three things cluttered the otherwise-empty room. Two massive light-blue throw pillows, a stack of books and magazines, and an old floor lamp with a ripped and battered lamp shade. Nadia had thrown another silk scarf over the lamp to hide the shade. This one had a reproduction of a famous Picasso painting on it. Faded lace curtains hung at the windows, and the impressive brick fireplace still held the winter ashes. He slowly made his way over to the mantel and picked up what appeared to be the only trivial item in the room, an eight-inch cheap metal souvenir replica of the Statue of Liberty. He turned it over and read the inscription on the bottom of the statue: "*Give me your tired, your poor, your huddled masses yearning to breathe free . . .*" He heard Nadia softly treading down the stairs and gently replaced the statue on the mantel. Nadia and her family had come to America searching for freedom, and by the look of the empty house they weren't planning on staying in Crow's Head, North Carolina, to find it.

Nadia was halfway down the stairs when she spotted Owen. "Oh, there you are, Mr. Prescott."

"My father was called Mr. Prescott. I'm Owen."

"*Was* Mr. Prescott?"

"My parents passed away about six years ago in a plane crash."

To lose both father and mother was terrible; to lose both at the same time was tragic. "I'm sorry." She gently touched his forearm with her fingers.

"Thank you." He could see her sadness and feel the comfort in her touch. He tenderly captured her fingers and gave them a gentle squeeze. A simple act of consolation ignited a bonfire. Heat scorched his fingers and raced up his arm.

Nadia's eyes widened a fraction before she jerked her trembling hand out from underneath Owen's. She quickly slid it into the deep pocket of her skirt. With the other hand she held out the money. "Here is the rest of your aunt's money."

He shook his head. "I don't want the money, Nadia." He glanced around the empty room. "You need it more than my aunt does."

She stubbornly continued to hold out the money. "Kandrataviches don't accept charity, Owen."

"Don't look on it as charity, then. Consider it a loan."

"I already owe the Prescotts enough." She thrust the bills into his hands.

Owen had held out his hand to push the money away but ended up with it anyway. "I don't understand. I've never loaned you any money."

"Prescotts sold me this ranch."

He held the money out to her. "Just because Prescott Realty acted as the realtor doesn't mean you owe them money. I'm sure everything was concluded on the day you made the settlement."

"Yes, that is true, but Prescott Mortgage Company holds the deed to this ranch." She cocked her head and studied Owen's baffled expression. "Don't you know what properties you own?"

"Yes. No." He glared at the money in his hand as if he'd never seen a dollar before. "I mean, I don't know." Now he was really confused. From all appearances Nadia and the rest of her family couldn't afford to pay the mortgage on a ranch of this size. He'd known the ranch was in run-down condition when it was placed on the market and how excited Don Adamson had been when it finally sold after two years. But how did Nadia get the mortgage past Bill Meyers? The manager of the Prescott Mortgage Company ran the place with an eye on the bottom line at all times. "The mortgage company doesn't own the ranch, Nadia; you do. We just lent you the money to buy it, that's all."

"You hold the papers that say it is mine." She slowly started to walk toward the kitchen with Owen.

"Only until you pay off the loan."

"Then it's not mine."

"Technically, yes, but—"

"And can't you sell the ranch to someone else?"

"Not unless you default on the loan." Owen groaned. "Didn't they explain all this to you when you applied for the mortgage?"

"Yes. Mr. Meyers was quite clear. For twenty years I make payments, then I get the papers. Until then you own part of the ranch."

Owen gazed into her intelligent, stubborn eyes and groaned again. Everything she said was true, but other people didn't look at their mortgage company as part-owner of their homes. "What about your parents? I'm sure they could explain that I don't own any part of the ranch."

"They never had a mortgage." A smile teased the corner of her mouth at the thought of her parents having a payment book.

"What about your uncles?"

Nadia's smile grew into a full-blown grin. "This is the first piece of property that a Kandratavich has ever owned."

"Ever?" cried Owen.

"Ever," answered Nadia with pride. She glanced around her kitchen and smiled. "I offered my good fortune to my family, and they have accepted." She frowned momentarily as she opened the door for him. "I'm afraid there's a lot they don't understand about the American way of life. Most of their information comes from old movies they watched while waiting for their visas."

"Let me guess." He ran his hand over his throat. "Were any of them old cowboy movies?" He didn't want to leave just yet.

Nadia fought the blush stealing up her cheeks as she remembered the mock hanging. "I guess I should warn you that my father and uncles watched every cowboy movie they could get their hands on."

"Great." Owen rubbed the back of his neck and wondered if he should warn the town sheriff about the Kandratavich gang.

"My brothers Stevo and Mikol favored Mel Gibson in *Lethal Weapon* and Kevin Costner in *Bull Durham*."

"This is getting better by the minute."

"My sister Sonia and her husband, Gustavo, became obsessed with Errol Flynn. My brother, Nikita, idolizes Cary Grant, and my other brother, Gibbie, thinks he's Elvis on spring break."

Owen studied Nadia's gorgeous face while waiting for the punch line. There had to be a joke somewhere in there. The most intriguing woman who had ever entered his life was living with the entire Actors Guild. "Exactly how many members of your family are living here, Nadia?" He glanced out of the open screen door and spotted two of her uncles working on the corral fence.

"Counting myself?"

"Sure."

"Thirty-one."

Owen silently groaned. The chances of finding Nadia alone at home were about as good as hitting the lottery. Curiously he asked, "What movies did *you* watch?"

"I've been living in the United States for five years now. My illusions about America vanished a long time ago." She walked out onto the porch and waved at her uncles.

Owen stood on the porch and saw his car off in the distance where he had parked it earlier. Why did she have to sound so sad when she mentioned vanishing illusions? Who had crushed her dreams? He jammed the money into his pocket. Now was not the time to argue about it. There were too many questions about Nadia and her family that needed answering first, and he knew just the place to find some of those answers: the Prescott Mortgage Company.

He reached out and took her hand on the pretense of shaking it. A small, jubilant smile teased his lips when he felt the slight trembling in her fingers. He had not imagined it; she was feeling it too. "Good-bye, Nadia. It's been an experience meeting your family and a definite pleasure meeting you." He tenderly ran his finger over her wrist and felt the rapid pounding of her pulse.

"Are you going to press charges against them?" The violent trembling in her fingers had to be from the fear she felt for her family, didn't it?

"Should I?" His grip tightened, and his gaze bore into hers.

"That wasn't my question."

He glanced over to the corral and encountered the hostile glares from her uncles. Could he in good conscience leave without doing something about the Kandrataviches? He owed the people of Crow's Head more consideration than that. "Will you talk to them about selling bottled water to unsuspecting folks?"

"I promise to give them such a lecture that their ears will blister."

"While you are at it, could you cover the topic of hanging one's neighbors?"

"I'll put hanging before swindling." She was going to give her family more than blisters on their ears. How did they ever expect to get jobs and become respectable members of the community if they acted like outlaws?

Her serious expression pulled at his heart. Her shoulders didn't look broad enough to carry the weight of her entire family, but they were. He released her hand and slowly raised his fingers to her forehead. With a tender stroke he smoothed out the worry wrinkle marring the graceful brow. He wanted to pull her into his arms and comfort her. His gaze locked in on her sweet mouth. Correction: He wanted to pull her into his arms and kiss her worries away. "Then I guess I won't be stopping at the sheriff's office on the way home."

Nadia released the breath she had been holding. "Thank you, Mr. Pres—I mean Owen."

He stepped off the porch before he could change his mind and kiss her anyway. There was work to be done, and if her uncles' glares were any indication, her family could use some cooling-off time. "Try to keep them out of trouble." He turned and headed for his car.

Nadia leaned against one of the peeling porch's posts and allowed herself the luxury of watching him stroll away. She usually thought jeans were the sexiest pants a man could wear, but the gray dress pants accenting Owen's rear did a superb job. Was it the pants or the man under them that she found so fascinating? She bit the inside of her cheek as he walked away. She should be congratulating herself for her magnificent acting job. Not once that she was aware of did she drool, gape, or sigh over his gorgeous body. It had been years since she last enjoyed the intimacy of a lover's caress or the pure satisfaction of mutual pleasure, but she knew potential when it landed on her front doorstep. And Owen J. Prescott radiated more potential than she knew what to do with.

Why, after all these years, did her hormones have to kick in, especially with Owen? He was the town's golden boy, the perfect southern gentleman, and she was entirely wrong for him. With a heavy sigh of regret she pushed away from the post and reentered the house. Why was it that you always hungered for what you couldn't have?

TWO

Owen softly closed the file after reading it a second time. He now understood Bill Meyers's decision to grant Nadia a mortgage. Not only had she put two thirds of the money down on the ranch but her collateral was a lucrative music contract. Nadia Kandratavich was on her way to becoming a famous international singer.

An hour ago he had caught Bill just as he was locking up the office for the evening. Bill had graciously offered to stay and answer any questions, but Owen had insisted Bill go on home to his wife and family, hastily assuring the man this had nothing to do with the way Bill was running the mortgage company. In the years since he had inherited the numerous businesses, Owen had purposely stayed out of the picture and let the managers run them, unless his opinion was asked for. His days were spent doing what he loved to do, designing buildings and homes and keeping his fingers in the running of his own construction company.

He leaned back and propped his feet up on Bill's desk as he glanced out of the office window overlooking the town square. The setting sun was gleaming off the bronze statue of his great-great-grandfather, General Jeremiah Prescott. Old Jeremiah would have had a fit if he could see what his great-great-grandson had done. A proper southern gentleman never invaded a young woman's privacy. Owen laced his fingers behind his neck and grinned. Then again, maybe old Jeremiah would have understood. After the Civil War Jeremiah had defied society and married a part-Cherokee maiden named Morning Eyes.

Owen glanced once more at the brown folder he had tossed onto the desk. Nadia was still shrouded in mystery. Why did she leave New York, where she was singing in a nightclub that paid her an astronomical salary, to move to a small, out-of-the-way town like Crow's Head? The nearest nightclub was in Asheville, a good thirty-five miles away. The contract had specified that Nadia was to write and record an album in four different languages by the end of the year. There was even an option for a considerable amount of money if she could produce the same album in two more languages by December 31. Nadia either had one hell of a job cut out for herself or she was fluent in at least six languages besides English. The part that really baffled Owen was that the contract called for songs that a renowned nightclub singer from New York wouldn't even think of singing. The album was to be a children's record with a title song called, "Animals Under My Bed."

With a heavy sigh Owen stood up and placed the file back into the cabinet. Some of his questions had been answered, but now there were twice as many others. He glanced at his watch as he hurriedly locked the office and got into his car. Tonight was Aunt Verna's bridge night, and with any luck he could make it home and into his office before any of her lady friends cornered him about eligible nieces and granddaughters. Sometimes he thought Verna's Thursday-night bridge club was an elaborate front for Matchmakers Anonymous.

Nadia stubbornly glared at her aunt Sofia and shook her head. She could think of a thousand ways to spend her Saturday; this was not one of them. "I don't want my tea leaves read."

Sofia pushed the antique bone-china cup across the counter toward Nadia. "You must." The cup had been in her family for generations, and she had lovingly held it in her lap during the entire flight to her new home in America. "Your mother had the dream again last night."

"Mama always has dreams."

"This is the sixth time she has had this same dream." She pushed the cup closer to Nadia's fingers. "Drink. Let me put her mind to rest."

"How can you put her mind to rest when she doesn't even know what the dreams mean?" Nadia's fingers lightly grazed the cup and saucer. Years before, Sofia had read her leaves and predicted a move of great distance for the entire family. Nadia had foolishly thought they would be leaving Russia and heading for Germany, Poland, or some other Eastern European country. Who would have thought six years ago that they all would be living in America?

"She knows the dreams concern you. She's afraid her love for her oldest child will cloud her judgment."

Nadia couldn't resist teasing her aunt, who was like a second mother to her. "Don't you feel any love for me, Sofia?"

"Foolish questions deserve no answers. Now, drink."

Nadia picked up the cup and glared at her aunt over the top of it. "I don't want to hear about any tall, dark, and handsome strangers."

Sofia placed her hands on her well-endowed hips as Nadia drank the tea. "I only say what I see, nothing more."

Nadia finished all but the dregs of the tea. With a triumphant smile she turned the cup over onto the saucer. "You will find only music, hard work, many responsibilities, and great happiness there." She purposely pushed the image of Owen Prescott from her mind. It was bad enough the man plagued her dreams—must he intrude on her every waking thought too?

Sofia waited a couple of moments for the liquid to drain out of the cup before slowly turning it back over. She carefully carried the cup over to the light pouring in from the window. With both hands cradling the cup, she stood there staring down into it.

Nadia's fingers absently tapped along with the music playing in her head. It was the song she had been working on for the past two days, the one she forcibly repeated over and over to block out any wayward thoughts of the tall, dark, and handsome Owen. The song was about a crocodile with a toothache and how no one wanted to help him for fear of being eaten.

"He will be carrying a gift," said Sofia, looking at her niece.

"Who?" Nadia had a sinking feeling she already knew.

Sofia sadly shook her head. "Foolish questions deserve no answers." She gazed back into the cup.

"I thought I told you I didn't want to hear about any tall, dark, handsome strangers. Save it for the *gadjos* when they plop down their money."

"I didn't say anything about him being tall, dark, or handsome." Sofia looked up and grinned "Besides, he's not a stranger any longer."

Nadia took the saucer over to the sink and carefully rinsed it. "This is what my mother's dreams had been about? Romantic foolishness." Foolishness was all it could ever be. Owen Prescott was a highly respectable man, the crowning son of Crow's Head— and totally out of her reach.

"No." Sofia moved away from the window and its light. "I see what your mother sees." She gazed at her niece with love and sadness. "The music stops."

Nadia's hands froze as she was drying the saucer. "What do you mean, the music stops?" The color drained from her face. Everyone knew how important her music was to her and to the family. "My music?"

"Yes, your music." Sofia rinsed the cup and carefully took the saucer from Nadia's trembling hands.

"Do I get it back?" demanded Nadia.

"I couldn't see."

"When does it go?"

"I couldn't see."

"Does *he* take it from me?"

Sofia shrugged her shoulders and gently replaced the cup and saucer in the velvet-lined wooden box her great-grandfather had made over a century ago. Her hesitation seemed to be hiding something. "I couldn't see."

"Could my mother see?" Her mother, Olenka, and her three aunts were as close as any family could be without being born of the same mother. The four Kandratavich brothers had counted their blessings more than once that all their wives got along so well, considering that they all lived as one family. They had also cursed many a time when the women stuck together and demanded their way. Olenka would have surely told Sofia everything that had happened in the dreams.

"No, her vision was blocked also."

"That's why she sent you over, isn't it? Everyone is afraid I will fail and lose the ranch." She walked over to the kitchen door and stared out through the screen. Uncles Yurik and Rupa were still working on the fencing of the corral. It was a difficult task made nearly impossible by the lack of proper materials. Nadia had persuaded her entire family to give up everything they knew and loved in Europe and to follow her dream of starting a new life in America. One that wasn't dominated by wars not of their making, one that knew no hunger but only a life of freedom. Had it all been a mistake?

"No one is afraid you will fail, Nadia." Sofia stood silently beside her and gazed out at her husband, Rupa, as he nailed a board into a fence post. "The ranch is our home too. We all must work hard to make it prosper. You have done more than your share, child."

Nadia cringed. At twenty-eight she was only five years younger than Sofia. "I haven't been a child for years, Sofia. When will you accept that fact?"

"When you hold your first babe against your breast," teased Sofia. She studied the younger woman's face. "If you are that worried about the music, I will send Yelena over to look at your hand."

"If I wanted my baby sister to read my palm, I would go to her."

"Yelena is nineteen, a full-grown woman, no?"

"No. There is much for her to learn yet." Nadia

glanced at her aunt. "Why is she a woman, and I still a child?"

"Because you are more fun to tease." Sofia hugged her niece. "Your sister could answer many of your questions. The gift is heavy with her."

"I know." Yelena's skill at reading palms would be remarkable if it wasn't downright frightening. Nadia had thanked her lucky stars *she* didn't possess any fortune-telling capabilities. Her first and only love was her music. Her fingers and the music that played constantly in her head were treasured gifts that she cherished beyond all else. "My losing the music could be anything from a sore throat to my death."

Sofia muttered a prayer and clutched the gold crucifix hanging from a chain around her neck. "Don't say such a thing."

Nadia chuckled and hugged her aunt. "Now who is teasing whom?"

Before Sofia could answer, a car slowly made its way up the rutted drive. Both women recognized Owen Prescott's shiny red car, but only Nadia recognized it for what it was, an American classic. Sofia raised one eyebrow as the candy-apple-red '65 convertible Mustang stopped in front of the house. "He'll have a gift."

"If we're all lucky, it won't be the sheriff," said Nadia. She was torn between her different, warring emotions. The woman inside her was delighted to see Owen again and was ready to run outside to greet him. The serious side of her nature was fearful that

Owen had indeed brought the sheriff and warrants for everyone's arrest. Only two days had passed since her uncles and father tried to hang the man.

Sofia smiled as Owen got out of the car, reached into the backseat, and pulled out a huge donkey made out of brightly colored paper. "See, the leaves were right." She opened the door and stepped out onto the porch.

Owen struggled momentarily under the weight of the papier-mâché donkey as he staggered toward the porch. When he had ordered the piñata from a novelty shop in Charlotte, he had requested that the donkey be packed with as much candy and small prizes as it would hold—he wanted Nadia's family's first experience with a piñata to be a memorable one. He was being rewarded for his efforts with a hernia and a jackass that was going to take a crane to be hoisted off the ground.

Nadia resisted the impulse to dash upstairs to change her clothes and run a brush through her hair. This morning she had taken IRS out for his daily run and hadn't yet found the time to change out of her faded jeans and skimpy lavender top. Her hair had been neatly braided at one time this morning, but the exuberance of the run had surely left its mark. Nadia watched through the screen as the muscles in Owen's forearms bulged under the strain of the colorful animal. She had no idea what Owen did all day, but whatever it was, he did more than sit behind some desk and push a pencil.

Owen carefully stood the three-foot-high donkey on the porch and took a deep breath. The papier-mâché animal felt as if it were steel-reinforced. Maybe the kids could use a baseball bat and smash the sucker open on the porch. He didn't think he had the strength to lift it again. He politely smiled at the woman standing on the porch and nodded his head: "Ma'am." He turned his attention to the screen door and the woman standing behind it. She was standing in the shadows, but he would have recognized her silhouette anywhere. She had haunted his dreams for the past two nights and had been the object of at least two very exotic daydreams. The little Gypsy angel had caused him to have some very uncomfortable moments. "Are you coming out, Nadia, or do I have to haul the piñata inside?" His smile held the combined charm of a southern gentleman and little boy. "I have to warn you, though, when the kids smash it open, it will make a mess."

Nadia opened the door and stepped onto the sun-drenched porch. She frowned at the multicolored donkey. "Won't he be ruined if you smash him open?"

"That's the general idea. His insides are filled with candies and small prizes. When he breaks open, all the kids scramble for the gifts."

"How do you open him?" questioned Nadia.

"You blindfold a child, give him a big stick, spin him around in a couple of circles to make him dizzy, and then let him try to smash the donkey." Owen patted the donkey on top of its head. "If the first kid fails to split him open after a couple of tries, you blindfold the next kid. You keep going until someone eventually breaks him open. Then it's a free-for-all on the goodies."

Nadia bit her lower lip. "He would be ruined."

"That's the idea, Nadia." Owen glanced between the donkey and her worried expression. "He's only made out of paper and some gluey stuff. When all the candy is out of him, he's toast."

"Breakfast?" asked a horrified-looking Sofia.

"No, Sofia, he means the donkey will be trash. 'Toast' is also slang for 'garbage.'" Nadia looked up at Owen. "Why would anyone want to smash a perfectly good donkey?" She ran her hand over the lumpy animals back and smiled. Chunks of red, blue, yellow, and purple paper tickled her fingers.

Owen shrugged his shoulders and frowned at the donkey. "That's the fun of it." He glanced at two of Nadia's uncles, who were making their way toward the porch. He couldn't tell by their expressions if he was about to become fish bait or be welcomed. His muscles tensed ready for action as they stepped onto the wooden porch.

Rupa and Yurik took off their hats and grinned at Owen. "Welcome, friend." Both men held out their hands.

Owen cautiously shook the first man's hand and glanced questioningly at Nadia. Someone had done some heavy-duty lecturing on American hospitality during the past two days.

"Hello, I am Rupa Kandratavich, and this is my

wife, Sofia." He nodded at the woman on the porch. "Welcome to our home, Mr. Prescott."

"Thank you. Please call me Owen." He released Rupa's hand and shook the huge hand of the man who looked like he could wrestle Godzilla and win.

"I am Yurik Kandratavich, and I also have a wife and many fine sons and daughters. Welcome to our home." He extended his hand.

Owen glanced at their clasped hands. This was not the gentle fist he remembered from Thursday. Was Yurik's wife one of the women he had accused of swindling his aunt Verna? "How do you do, Yurik?"

"I do well." Yurik beamed with pride at his mastery of the English language and shook Owen's hand vigorously.

Owen withdrew his hand from Yurik's overzealous handshake. "I can see that you do." He absently flexed his aching fingers. "I brought a gift for all the children to enjoy."

Both men glanced down at the gaudy donkey, nodded, and smiled pleasantly. "Thank you very much," said Rupa.

"They will get many hours of viewing pleasure from it," added Yurik.

Nadia chuckled at Owen's confused expression and decided to help him out. "It's a piñata, uncles. We need a place we can hang it from with plenty of room underneath."

"Will the tree by the barn do?" questioned Rupa.

Owen glanced at the huge oak tree and grimaced.

Did the Kandratavich brothers have a thing for hanging things from oak trees? But he replied, "It's perfect." He bent to pick up the heavy beast of burden.

Yurik saw the muscles strain across Owen's back and took the piñata from him.

Owen watched in astonishment as Yurik walked across the yard as if he were carrying a child's toy. He chuckled softly and said, "I know someone who eats his Wheaties for breakfast."

"Yes," said Sofia as she stepped off the porch to follow Yurik and her husband, "Along with orange juice, coffee, and garbage."

Nadia hid her laughter behind her hand and glanced at Owen from beneath lowered lashes. "I think she means toast." She lightly vaulted down the steps and looked back over her shoulder at Owen. "Are you coming?"

At the sound of her voice Owen slid his gaze away from the sweet curve of her denim-clad bottom and up until he encountered her laughing dark eyes. His fantasies hadn't done her justice. Nadia was even more irresistible than he had remembered. "I'm right behind you."

Owen felt Nadia shudder with each crack of the stick. So far only the smallest of the children had a whack at cracking the donkey, and to no avail. The older children were circled around the swinging piñata, well out of harm's way, ready to pounce in case a five-year-old boy named Zolly managed to succeed. Mothers were shouting encouragement, and fathers were placing bets on which child would smash the donkey open. Every member of the Kandratavich family had come to Sofia's summons, rung on an old metal triangle dangling by the side of the barn. Owen had seen towns with fewer people than the Kandratavich Ranch. He leaned closer to Nadia and half-teasingly whispered, "Are you sure everyone is here?"

She glanced around at the smiling faces of her family. Everyone appeared totally captivated with Owen's gift. "Of course everyone's here. Did you think we would start without someone?"

"No," chuckled Owen, "I was just wondering how you can tell." He moved closer and tried to place the scent of her shampoo. Whatever it was, it was driving him crazy. He wanted to snap the rubber band holding the end of the braid together, run his fingers through the thick mass of silk, and bury his face in the heavenly softness until he could place that elusive scent.

She smiled as a little dark-haired girl was given her turn. "They're family. When you grow up surrounded by them, you can tell when someone is missing."

"Never lost a child?" Owen grimaced as the little girl swinging the stick connected with Yurik instead of the donkey. The big man laughed and swung the squealing girl up into his arms. A dark-eyed boy with a determined look took her place under the blindfold.

"Only Mikol, my brother, but he never counted."

She nodded her head toward a young man in his mid-twenties who was dressed in a pair of jeans and a white T-shirt.

"Why didn't he count?"

"Mikol could never be found. At first we thought he was playing with us when he used to disappear— you know, the kid's game peekaboo."

"You mean hide-and-seek." Another boy, slightly older than the last one, got his turn. Owen knew it wouldn't be long now before the piñata was smashed.

"Yes, that's the one." Nadia glanced at her brother with sadness and love. "He has the true heart of a Gypsy."

Owen glanced around in confusion at the smiling faces of her family. "I thought you are all of Gypsy descent?"

"We are," said Nadia proudly, "but Mikol wanders. When he was a little boy, he wandered away from the camp all the time. By the time he was fifteen, he had run away from home more times than we could count. When he turned sixteen, he headed out on his own for good. He only rejoined the family to make America his home."

"Couldn't your parents stop him?"

"It would be like trying to stop the wind. Mikol is who he is. We are each different from one another, and we must accept our individual fate."

Owen could feel the excitement surrounding the game increase. The cheering and shouting were growing louder. The older boys were now getting their turns at the donkey. He ignored the furor and concentrated on the sadness lurking in Nadia's dark eyes. His fingers reached out and gently brushed back a dark stream of her hair blowing lightly in the summer breeze. It was softer than he had imagined. His voice was barely a whisper as he asked faintly, "What are you made of, Nadia?"

"Music, responsibilities"—liquid darkness shimmered in the depths of her eyes as she gazed up at Owen—"and badness."

His eyes opened fractionally in surprise as total pandemonium broke out. Someone had finally succeeded in breaking open the piñata. Brightly colored plastic-wrapped candies and small, inexpensive children's toys flew in every direction from the wildly swinging donkey. The adults cheered as the kids dived for the goodies. *Badness! Nadia had said she was made up of badness. What in the hell did that mean?*

Nadia bent down and picked up a couple pieces of candy and a plastic-beaded necklace and handed them to her three-year-old cousin, who was having trouble getting around some of the older kids. "Here you go, sweetie." She pointed to some candy that had landed farther out, which none of the other children had seen. The little girl grinned and toddled off. Nadia slowly stood back up and faced Owen.

He had followed her every motion with the child. If there was an ounce of badness in Nadia, he was Jack the Ripper. A smile teased the outside corner of his mouth. "That was a heartless thing to do, Nadia."

He forced the smile down. "Helping a poor innocent child get some candy. Shame on you."

"I didn't say I was heartless."

"Just bad, right?"

A touch of red darkened her face. "Right."

Owen couldn't help himself. He burst out laughing. "You couldn't be bad if someone drew you a diagram and showed you how." He admitted that he really didn't know Nadia very well, but his instincts had never failed him yet. Nadia looked three-fourths angel, one-fourth temptress.

"You have no idea what you are talking about." She quickly turned away, only to bump directly into her father.

Milosh steadied his daughter and grinned at Owen. "Hello, my new friend named Owen."

Owen smiled and forced his gaze away from the lovely black-and-blue eye Milosh was sporting. A shiner he had given the man. "Hello, my new friend named Milosh."

Milosh slapped him on the back. "You stay for dinner. We have much food."

His smile turned into a full-blown grin as he saw Nadia stiffen. He had won over her family with the piñata, but for some reason she was trying to scare him away with a ridiculous story about badness. Hadn't she realized that instead of scaring him she had made him more curious? His gaze locked directly with Nadia's. "I will be honored to join you and the rest of the *family*, Milosh."

THREE

Nadia glanced from beneath lowered lashes at the man silently walking beside her in the growing dusk. Owen was a paradox. He was a man of great wealth, obviously used to eating from tables draped in fine linen tablecloths and sporting expensive china and matching silverware. Yet tonight he had sat at a rough wooden table on crude wooden benches and fit right in with the rest of her family. He had cleared his plate twice, much to the delight of her mother and aunts, and had complimented them outrageously. Owen Prescott couldn't have better won over her family if the heavens had opened up and deposited him smack in the middle of their camp.

She had expected him to be offended by the sight of the Kandratavich camp. Material possessions never dominated a Gypsy's life. Her family enjoyed the freedom of their old life and saw no reason to change when they started over in America. Nadia had spent a small fortune to have the family's four *vardos* shipped across the Atlantic and freighted to North Carolina. The brightly painted horse-drawn wagons now stood under giant oaks in a picturesque valley on the ranch. They were the center of the camp. She had also persuaded her family to allow her to purchase two secondhand mobile homes that provided them with heat, running water, and bathrooms. Life in the Kandratavich camp would be considered hard, if not primitive, by most people's standards, but her family felt they were living in the lap of luxury.

"You're awfully quiet," said Owen. The fading light was making it difficult to see, but he could feel the tension radiating from her.

Nadia worried her lower lip and ducked under a cracked board that at one time was part of a fence enclosing the pasture they had just walked through. She felt uneasy walking the fields at twilight with Owen. It felt too familiar, too intimate, to be heading for her home just over the next hill. "Sorry." In another five minutes he would be gone, and she'd be safely in her room writing down the song she'd been hearing in her head all evening, about a colorful donkey who had run away from home so he wouldn't have to be a piñata.

Owen followed her under the fence. "Can I ask a question?"

"Sure."

"What exactly was in the stew? I recognized a couple of unusual leaves in the salad that would have given Aunt Verna's garden club hysterics, but some of the ingredients were totally unfamiliar."

"Do you really want to know?"

Owen hesitated at the sound of amusement in her voice. "Let me rephrase that. Should I be worried about what I just ate?"

"Not unless you're a vegetarian." She laughed softly at his look of uneasiness. "Relax, Owen. Just because I've never seen that particular dish on any menu in America doesn't mean it was an endangered species or anything." She stopped at the top of the hill and glanced down at the weathered barn and plain house. No matter how many times she climbed this hill and admired the view, her heart always cried out the same message: She was home. "You did enjoy it, didn't you?"

"Almost as much as the company." His gaze was focused on her stunning profile.

Nadia ignored the compliment in his voice. "Thank you again for being so understanding with my father and uncles."

"They're a great bunch of guys when they aren't trying to hang someone." He chuckled softly as he remembered how obsessed Rupa had become during their discussion on the "code of the West." The man had actually thought cattle rustling was still the number-one offense in America.

Nadia was thankful that the dusk obscured the flush stealing up her face. "I appreciate your not pressing charges."

"It wasn't entirely their fault. If I remember correctly, I did come on a little strong." He smiled sheepishly. "I guess we have that in common."

She passed the barn and purposely headed for his car. She didn't want to know what they had in common. Every instinct born into her—Gypsy, human, and especially woman—was screaming to get away from him. Owen was trouble. Man trouble. And if there was anything more she didn't need in her life right now, it was more trouble.

"We both care very deeply for our family."

"Well, of course I care about my family," cried Nadia. "Doesn't everybody?"

"No." He leaned against the front bumper of his car and glanced over to her house. "Have I done something to offend you, Nadia?"

"Of course not. Why do you ask?" She shifted her weight from her left foot to her right and nervously toyed with the gold necklace hanging around her neck. Three crystals bit into the softness of her palm.

"Then I must make you uneasy." His relaxed position against the car didn't change.

Nadia released the necklace and silently listened to the song whirling around in her head. The music was still there. He had not taken her gift. She slowly smiled at her own foolishness. How could he possibly take away her music? "I am not afraid of you."

"Good." His brilliant smile flashed in the growing darkness. "Then will you have dinner with me tomorrow night?"

"I . . ." She glanced around wildly, trying to think up an excuse he would accept without taking offense.

"Dinner, Nadia, that's all I'm asking." He saw

the look of panic that had flashed in her eyes. "Your aunt thinks you have been working too hard."

"Which aunt?" Nadia ground her teeth on a curse that would surely invoke a lightning attack from above.

"Sofia." He had been pleased by her family's obvious attempts at matchmaking. "Your mother mentioned that you haven't been out since they arrived five months ago."

Stifling a curse, she asked, "What else did my 'well-meaning' family say?" If she wasn't so damn mad, she would have crawled under a rock and died of mortification.

"It wasn't their fault." He jammed his hands into the pockets of his jeans. "I kind of pumped them for information."

"Why?"

"Because you've been avoiding me since the piñata was broken open. At first I thought you might already have a boyfriend, but Sofia said no; only your music keeps you warm at night."

"Sofia ought to mind her own business," snapped Nadia.

Owen glanced down at his feet to hide his smile. "She loves you, and so do the others." He eyed the stubborn angle of her jaw. "They're afraid you're becoming a stick-in-the-mud."

"Stick-in-the-mud?" shouted Nadia. After everything she had done for them, everything she had sacrificed, how could they say that? For months all she could think about were the songs for the album. Everything she did, she did with music playing in her mind. She ate, walked, and slept music. All for them. All to be called a stick-in-the-mud.

He chuckled. "Your mother's exact words were 'twig-in-the-dirt,' but I got the picture."

Nadia saw red and allowed her temper to overrule her common sense. "What time will you pick me up?" She'd show them who was a stick-in-the-mud. The way her family was throwing her at him, she was amazed her father hadn't sat down with him and worked out a marriage contract. Hell, she must be worth at least three good horses and a small sack of gold coins.

Owen parked the car in front of Nadia's house at precisely one minute to seven the following evening. He felt like a heel. He never should have goaded her into having dinner with him. The only excuse he could come up with during a sleepless night was desperation. She had been avoiding him all afternoon, purposely putting little children and anyone else she could find between them yesterday. If he had wanted to talk to her during dinner last night, he would have had to use a bullhorn or walkie-talkies. Nadia had made sure he was at the opposite end of the Kandratavich dinner table with at least thirty people between them. He had known she was going to refuse his dinner invitation before he'd even asked. For some reason she was running from the sparks they struck off each other.

He glanced in the rearview mirror and made sure his tie was straight before picking up the small bouquet of wildflowers and getting out of the car. His footsteps were heavy and slow as he climbed the two steps to the porch and knocked on the door. He wouldn't blame her one bit if she'd changed her mind.

Nadia heard the knock and swallowed the lump in her throat. Three times this morning she had picked up the telephone in the kitchen and dialed his number to cancel this date, only to hang up before the last digit had been pressed. The truth of the matter was, she might have accepted the date to prove something to her family, but she was keeping the date because she wanted to. Owen was everything she had always looked for in a man. He was confident, intelligent, liked children, and was handsome. He could turn her knees into water with just one look and cause a riot of excitement to skip down her spine with only the slightest of touches. He was also more than three years too late.

She took a last glance in the mirror and pushed back a wayward curl. She couldn't change history, but she could enjoy this one night. Who knew, maybe Owen would give her the last song she needed for the album. He had already provided the inspiration for the adorable little number about José, the paper donkey. She picked up the small clutch purse from the crowded dresser top and walked out of the bedroom, turning off the light behind her.

Owen smiled and straightened the clear plastic wrap the florist had placed around the colorful bouquet of flowers as Nadia opened the door. For a minute there he thought no one was going to answer his knock. He stepped into the kitchen, and his pleasant smile turned into a whistle of appreciation as his gaze caressed every one of Nadia's curves. He had known Nadia was beautiful and had a body that could stop a freight train, but this woman standing before him could tame a lion without using a whip. Not only was her dress a mind-boggling red, but it clung to each curve like a pair of lover's hands. He swallowed heavily as his gaze slid over red high heels, up past the sexiest pair of legs he had ever had the pleasure to meet, over gently flaring hips, trim waist, and a generously endowed bustline. A fine gold chain lay against the satiny smoothness of her throat, drawing his gaze upward to the sweet temptation of her ripe mouth and the fire carefully blanketed in the depths of her dark eyes. He watched entranced as her pearly-white teeth sank into the sweet fullness of her lower lip.

His soft moan caused his body to rebel against the lack of oxygen. He had forgotten to breathe at the sight of Nadia. He hastily covered his tactlessness with a cough. The trembling of his fingers was barely detectable as he handed Nadia the flowers. "Lord, you are beautiful."

"Thank you." Nadia clutched the bouquet. "Is this dress appropriate? You didn't say where we were going." She had only a handful of sophisticated dresses, which were purchased when she arrived in America and started singing in nightclubs. Most had been bought in secondhand shops and had satisfied the owners' ideas of what a singer should wear.

The closet in one of the spare bedrooms was jam-packed with sequined gowns with no back, very little front, and slits that started at the floor and ended at mid-hip. They were from another life, and all bore the stamp of her disgrace. The closet door had been nailed shut and would stay that way.

Owen pulled at the knot in his tie and tried to swallow. He'd rather cut off his right arm than tell her to change her dress. "You look perfect." It was the understatement of the year.

Nadia lowered her gaze to the flowers in her hands and mumbled another polite "Thank you."

"You're welcome." He smiled at the blush staining her cheeks. "Why don't you put them in some water? They'll last longer that way."

She crinkled the clear plastic between her fingers. "I wasn't thanking you for the flowers, I was . . ."

Owen raised an eyebrow. "You don't like the flowers."

"Of course I do. They're beautiful." She walked over to the cabinet above the stove and pulled out an empty glass jar and filled it with water. "Thank you." She carefully unwrapped the flowers and slowly placed them in the jar, one flower at a time. She glanced out from underneath her lashes at the handsome man standing in her kitchen watching her every move. A purple iris tumbled from her fingers and landed on the counter. She quickly picked it up and jammed it into the jar. His intense gaze was making her jittery. Her insides were beginning to feel like a chocolate bar that had been left on the dashboard of her car in July. She placed the last sprig of baby's breath into the jar and tossed the wrapping into the garbage can under the sink. "Are you ready?"

He was ready for a lot of things. Walking out that door wasn't one of them. "Sure." He held open the door for her. "Aren't you bringing a wrap?"

"No, summer evenings are to enjoy, not to be hidden from." She flipped on the porch lights as she left the house.

Owen closed the door behind them and admired the view of Nadia's retreating form as she walked toward his car. He sent a silent prayer heavenward, thankful that Nadia didn't believe in hiding. The view captivating his attention was guaranteed to make this one of the warmest summer nights he'd ever encountered.

Nadia smiled politely at the young man holding the car door open and stared at the imposing building in front of her. Huge white columns, lush greenery, floor-to-ceiling windows, and the gentle, seductive whispering of a massive fountain dominating the front lawn greeted her. Her heart sank. Owen was taking her to the most exclusive restaurant in five counties, the Foxchase Country Club. Only people with pedigrees dating back before the Civil War dined here—people with *old* money, who drank mint juleps on their verandas and had butlers to answer their doors. People like Owen.

She glanced around and watched as Owen, who had turned the car over to the valet, rounded the front bumper, and walked toward her. He was dressed in an immaculate dark gray suit, a crisp white shirt, and a conservative striped tie. He looked confident, rich, and extremely sexy. He looked as if he had just stepped off the cover of *GQ*, while she looked like she was about to lie across the top of a baby-grand piano and belt out some old Nat King Cole songs.

Owen tenderly took her elbow and led her up the few steps to the front door. A young man dressed in high-waisted black pants and a short jacket materialized out of nowhere and opened the door for them. Nadia felt the artificial coolness and shivered as they stepped into the foyer.

"Cold?" He had felt her shiver.

"No, it's just the sudden climate change." She glanced around the elegant room. Twelve-foot-high ceilings, crystal chandeliers, marble floors, and imported carpets dominated the room. Plants the size of small trees were the only splash of color against the sterile white walls. The first thing she would have done with the room was paint it fire-engine red or cobalt blue to brighten it up. Didn't the filthy rich believe in color?

"Monsieur Prescott, so nice to see you again." A man in his late fifties bowed first to Owen, then to Nadia. "Mademoiselle."

Owen chuckled, and lightly slapped the man on his back. "Cut it out, George. We both know you can't speak a word of French."

George glanced over his shoulder to make sure he couldn't be overheard. "Thaddeus will have my job if I don't greet the clientele right."

"Tell Thaddeus to stick this job and come work for me. The way you handle all these young men as they wait on tables, clear them off, park cars, and open doors, you'd be a perfect supervisor on the job site."

George beamed but shook his head. "Thanks for the offer, Mr. Prescott, but I'm getting too old to stand around a construction site all day in bad weather." He led the way out of the foyer and across the dining room to an intimate table set for two with a breathtaking view of the formal gardens and the golf course in the distance.

Nadia ignored the impressive view of the gardens, which were not as spectacular as some of the scenery found on her own ranch. She owned crystal-clear streams flowing with trout and water so pure you could drink it. There were meadows overflowing with wildflowers in a kaleidoscope of colors, and the majestic Smoky Mountains climbing halfway to heaven in the distance. Who would want to look at the well-manicured grass of a golf course when she had all that?

She glanced at Owen and started to relax for the first time that night. She had liked George and was pleased to see their table was partly hidden from the curious glances of the blue-blooded clientele by huge plants. "So that's what you do."

"What?"

"Work in construction. I was wondering how you stayed so fit." She flushed to the roots of her hair and took a hasty sip of water. *Why don't you just come right out and tell the man you've been drooling over his body?*

Owen grinned. "I don't believe it. Ms. Kandratavich actually paid me a compliment."

"I give compliments all the time." Her brows pulled together in a frown.

"Ah, but never to me." He was beginning to love the way she blushed. His gaze slid down her throat to the softly rounded neckline of her dress to where just a trace of cleavage showed, and he wondered exactly where the blush started. Were the softly rounded breasts concealed by her dress the same delicate pink as her throat? Would her nipples darken?

"Excuse me, sir."

Owen came back to earth with a thud. He glanced up at the waiter standing next to the table. "What?" he snapped.

The waiter held out a deep-red leather-bound menu. "I asked if the gentleman would like to see our wine list before ordering."

Owen took the wine list and willed away the flush that was stealing up his face. Never in all his years of dating had he sat in a restaurant and stared at his date's cleavage. For Lord's sake, he was a grown man, not some hormone-driven teenager on his first date. He glanced at the list, snapped it shut, and handed it back to the young waiter with an order for an expensive bottle of white wine.

"Thank you, sir."

Owen watched the waiter leave with a frown before jerking his gaze back to Nadia. "I'm sorry, Nadia." He felt the flush threaten to overcome him again. "Is wine all right, or would you prefer something else?" Where in the hell had all his social skills suddenly gone?

"Wine is fine." A smile teased the corner of her mouth at Owen's obvious discomfort. "I'm not much of a drinker. Two glasses of wine and I'd be standing on some table singing Neil Diamond numbers."

Owen chuckled at the mental pictures flashing through his mind. Half the ladies dining would faint dead away, the gentlemen would probably secretly cheer, and Foxchase Country Club would revoke his membership. He glanced around the stuffy room and realized he wouldn't have cared if they did. He only came here because of their great French chef and to please the haughty clients who were paying him outrageous sums to design their homes. Tonight he had brought Nadia, hoping to impress her with his style, wealth, and charm. It had been an error: He should have taken her to Belle's and showed her the best fried chicken this side of the Mason-Dixon Line.

He reached up and tugged at his tie. "Neil Diamond, hmmm?" His voice was teasing soft as he leaned across the table and whispered, "What would you do if you had three glasses?"

Nadia felt herself relax into the chair. This was the Owen she had wanted to get to know tonight. If she was only going to allow herself one date with him, she wanted it to be perfect. A wide grin spread across her face as she whispered back, "I'm told I do a great impersonation of Madonna."

Owen's rich laughter caused more than a few heads to turn and stare at the couple halfway hidden by lush green leaves.

Nadia leaned against the screen door and smiled up at Owen. "Thank you for a wonderful evening."

He placed one palm against the metal doorframe above her head while the fingers on the other hand gently played with a thick dark curl lying against her shoulder. "You're welcome." He tenderly cupped her chin and studied her face in the light illuminating the porch. Even under the harsh glare of the yellow bug light, she was breathtakingly beautiful. "Have dinner with me tomorrow?"

She tried to look away, but his fingers wouldn't release her chin. "I'm sorry, I can't."

"The next night?"

Nadia shook her head. "Please, Owen, don't."

"Don't what?" His brown eyes held nothing but confusion.

"Don't end this evening with an argument." She took a deep breath to calm her pounding heart. "You're very nice, Owen, and I had a wonderful time tonight."

"But?"

"I never should have accepted this date. It's all wrong."

"Why didn't you cancel it, then?"

"I tried three times." She glanced over his shoulder at the moon and the gentle swaying branches of the giant oaks in the distance. Her voice was barely above a whisper. "I couldn't bring myself to do it."

His fingers tenderly stroked the satiny texture of her cheek. "Why couldn't you?"

"To be perfectly honest with you, I find you extremely attractive." She frowned at the loose knot of Owen's tie and gathered all her strength. "I just can't see you again. It's too tempting."

His arms fell to his side, and he jammed both of his hands onto his hips. "Let me see if I've got this right. You aren't seeing anyone else, you find me *extremely* attractive, you had a wonderful time tonight, but you won't go out with me again."

It sounded stupid even to her own ears. She tried a new approach. "We just aren't meant for each other, Owen. I'm sorry."

He jammed his fingers through his hair and paced to the other end of the porch. He glanced toward the heavens and muttered either a curse or a prayer before storming his way back to her. His gaze locked on the delicate trembling of her lower lip. The same lip that had been tempting him all night with its lush redness and sweet promises.

Nadia felt her whole world shake as his finger gently traced her lower lip. She should leave and go into the house, but her feet weren't receiving the urgent message her brain was sending. The traitors were listening to her misguided heart. Heat scorched her lungs, making breathing an impossibility, as he moved closer. The forthcoming kiss was in his eyes. She could see its heat, practically taste its sweetness, and feel its power. She wanted that kiss. Even as her brain was shouting, *Run*, her body was leaning forward.

Owen tenderly cupped her face and lightly covered her mouth with his own. His body shook against the restraint he had forced upon it.

Nadia melted under his tender onslaught. Her hands rose of their own accord and encircled his neck. She pressed herself against his strength and deepened the kiss with a seductive stroke of her tongue. One moment he was as gentle as a newborn kitten, and the next, the untamed hunger of a wild lion broken free. Nadia reveled in the uncivilized side of Owen. She met him stroke for stroke, kiss for kiss. The more he demanded, the more she gave. Her breasts swelled with need, and liquid heat pooled in her stomach and overflowed to the juncture between her thighs.

She felt his warm hands tenderly cup her hips and pull her closer. A groan escaped her throat as his arousal pressed against the gentle swell of her abdomen. Hell itself couldn't generate this much heat. Passion throbbed between her legs as she broke the kiss and moaned his name. "Owen?"

He strung a line of kisses up her jaw to the edge of her ear. He nipped lightly at the delicate lobe and toyed with the small golden hoop earring with his breath. "How could you say we aren't meant for each other?"

Nadia lowered her head to his chest and willed the tears not to come. She could feel the rapid hammering of his heart through the white silk shirt and knew hers was just as fast. What had she done? She never should have kissed Owen. It could only complicate matters. She backed out of his arms and gripped the handle of the screen door behind her. She needed something to hold on to. "I'm sorry, Owen. That shouldn't have happened."

"But it did." His breathing was harsh, and his eyes glimmered with frustration. What was she running from? "You can't tell me you didn't feel it too."

Nadia kept her gaze pinned to his billowing chest as she pulled open the screen door and twisted the knob of the inner door. It was safer not to answer that question. "I have to go in now." The blackness of the kitchen engulfed her as she stepped over the threshold.

Owen gripped the frame of the screen door but didn't follow her in. "I'm not giving up, Nadia."

She sadly shook her head and started to close the door. "I won't change my mind."

He scowled at the closed door and muttered, "We'll see." How could she be so blind as not to see what was happening between them? He gently closed the screen door and thought. Whatever was bothering Nadia had to do with the mysterious comment she made yesterday about being bad. What could she possibly have done that was so terrible—cheat at tarot cards, fail crystal-ball reading, or misread someone's palm? Whatever it was, he just didn't care. He wasn't about to walk away from the best thing that had ever happened to him. He scowled once more at the closed door before walking back to his car and driving away.

Nadia heard his car pull away and wiped at the tears rolling down her cheeks. She had no right to feel sorry for herself. She knew it would never work from the beginning. It was better to end it now than later, when Owen would despise her. Her hand swiped at another tear. He had absolutely no right to kiss her like that. He was a southern gentleman and should have kissed like one, all stuffy and formal, not as sweet as heaven and hot as Hades.

She had more important things to think about than dream lovers and unquenched desires. She had her music. She leaned against the door, closed her eyes, and willed the music to soothe her tattered soul.

Five seconds later her eyes flew open. She glanced around the darkened kitchen, terrified. Her mind was a complete blank. There were no serene sounds or tranquil melodies. No magical lyrics or foot-tapping tunes bombarding her mind for a song of their own. There was only an emptiness. Her mother and Sofia had been right. The music had stopped. Owen had stolen her music.

FOUR

Owen glanced up from the stack of papers scattered across his desk as his study door opened. A huge grin spread across his face at the woman ducking under Sebastian's arm and sprinting into his office. "Nadia!" He jumped to his feet. She had come to him.

"Sir, I'm terribly sorry for this. . . ." said the embarrassed-looking butler.

"It's okay, Sebastian. Ms. Kandratavich is welcome anytime." Owen raised his eyebrows in astonishment at the woman standing in front of him. "How did you slip past Sebastian?" The butler had been with the family for more than thirty years, and she was the first person who had ever managed to make it past him. The stiff and imposing Sebastian had always reminded Owen of a formidable guard dog, but he obviously cared very deeply for Aunt Verna.

Nadia glanced at the stone-faced butler and offered a small smile. "I used one of your football plays. I faked left and went right."

Owen suppressed his chuckle as Sebastian bowed slightly to Nadia in acknowledgment and asked, "Is there anything else, sir?"

"No, that will be all. Thanks." He dismissed the butler and concentrated on the fiery woman in front of him. Her hair was long and flowing, and the flush of excitement tinted her cheeks with a warm glow. She looked vibrantly alive and happy. "Nadia?"

She turned to Owen's voice, and her smile instantly died. A fierce crease pulled at her brow, and she placed both hands flat on the desk and demanded, "I want it back, immediately!" Playing dodge-the-butler with the formidable-looking Sebastian had been fun, but now it was time to settle up on some business.

Owen blinked. "What back?"

Nadia clenched her teeth together and leaned in closer. "My music." Five days of total silence had driven her to this. Five days of nothing but eerie silence. Not one note, one fleeting melody, or one inspiring line of a cute lyric had crossed her mind in five endless days and sleepless nights. She had no idea how he'd taken it, only that he had. The music had been there during dinner, and even on the drive home she could remember the melodies mixing with the cool summer night's breeze and Owen's deep laughter over some silly story she had told him from her childhood. The music had been there until he had stolen it with a kiss.

"What music?"

She raised her voice and shouted, "My music." Was he deaf?

Owen frowned and sat down in the soft leather chair he had just vacated. "You lost your music, and you think I took it."

"I don't think, Owen, I know."

"When did you lose it?"

"I had it when I went to dinner with you the other night, but it was gone after you dropped me off."

He ran a tired hand over his face and thought. "Don't panic, Nadia. It has to be around somewhere. What was it, sheet music, a cassette, what?" He reached for the phone. "I'll call the restaurant and see if someone has found it." He started punching out numbers. "Maybe you dropped it in my car, and it slid under the seat." He jabbed the last number. "Why in the hell were you carrying something that valuable on you?" His voice trailed off as Nadia's finger reached over the desk and pushed the button to disconnect the phone call.

Nadia glanced at his puzzled expression and wondered how in the world she was going to explain about the music. With a heavy sigh she said, "Put down the phone, Owen. The music's not at the Foxchase Country Club." She slowly walked over to the French doors and stared out across the slate patio. Precision-cut hedges partially obscured the view of the sparkling swimming pool on the right, huge potted plants overflowed concrete urns, discreet benches dotted the lawn, and the high chain-link fence could be glimpsed off to the left, marking the tennis courts. Owen's home was more of a country club than Foxchase.

She pressed her forehead against the cool glass of the door and closed her eyes. "The music was in my head."

"If it was in your head, how did you lose it?"

"I wish I knew." Nadia sighed. She turned around and shrugged her shoulders. Nothing had gone right in the past five days. IRS had broken out of the corral twice, two great job prospects for her father and Uncle Rupa had fallen through, and this morning her mother had told her that her brother Mikol hadn't been seen in two days. The only thing she had accomplished in the past five days were some translations of a couple of other songs that were already written. It was a difficult and slow process, translating words to fit the same melody in six different languages, but she was bound and determined not only to fulfill the contract but to meet the option clause. The extra money could go a long way toward purchasing a used tractor for the ranch and acquiring a couple of brood mares for IRS to mate with. All that was missing was one last song. She had to get back the music before October, when she was supposed to start recording.

"How do you figure I'm the one who caused you to lose it?"

"Because it was there before you kissed me."

It took a moment before a huge grin lit up Owen's face, and his eyes sparkled with delight. "Are you saying that I kissed the music straight out of your head?"

She frowned at the gleam in his eye. He didn't have to look so damn pleased. Her chin tilted up an inch, and she held her ground as Owen stood up. "All I am saying is, it was there before you kissed me."

Owen tried to tamp down his grin but failed utterly. "I've never been accused of kissing someone's music away before."

"It wasn't just *music*, Owen. It is my livelihood"— her voice cracked with tension—"and the sole means of support for my entire family."

The grin vanished instantly. She wasn't joking. Whatever creative process was involved in her songwriting had been stopped. Her future as an international children's singer was in jeopardy. He took a couple of steps toward her and reached for her hand. "I'm sorry, Nadia. I don't mean to make light of the situation, but I'm having trouble connecting my kissing you to your losing the music in your head."

"If you think you're having a hard time, imagine it from my side. One simple dinner date, that's all it was supposed to be. No dancing, no dark movie theaters, nothing but food and conversation for a couple of hours." She glanced down at the intertwined fingers and frowned. Her hand looked so small and helpless compared with his. She wondered what it would feel like to allow Owen's strength to support her. She released his hand and took a safe step back away from the temptation. "I asked myself what could one date hurt?" She shrugged her shoulders and made a vain attempt to laugh at her own foolishness.

He leaned his hip against the side of the desk and tried to think logically. "Maybe what you are suffering from is writer's block?"

"I'm not a writer, Owen. I'm a musician. I hear music." She gestured wildly around the room with her hands. "Normally I could stand in this room and hear the music it plays for me."

"Rooms play music for you?"

Nadia glanced around the spacious study and groaned. "See the rich, dark wood?" She waved to the paneled walls and the floor-to-ceiling bookshelves. "They hum to me." She moved her hand toward the French doors. "The gentle sunlight streaming into the room makes a light, airy sound. Your desk would give off your presence, and the paperwork and blueprints will build in volume parroting what you do, you create and build." Her hands fell helplessly by her side in frustration. "Everything in this room would sing, hum, or serenade me."

"Won't it be hard to separate all the different sounds?"

"No." She relaxed slightly. At least he hadn't laughed. "It's just like decorating. The walls, the books, the desk, even the curtains—all pull together and create one room. When I listen, I hear one melody, created by all the things."

Owen glanced around his office in amazement. He never thought about music like that. Curiously he asked, "What do you hear now?"

Nadia followed his gaze and concentrated. She clasped her hands together in front of her and closed her eyes as tears flooded them. "I hear nothing but your voice." She slowly opened her eyes and willed the tears away.

He couldn't stand the look of total defeat etched into her face. Breaking his resolve not to crowd her, he gently pulled her into his arms and held her close. "Don't worry—we'll find your music."

Nadia allowed herself the luxury of relying on his strength for just one moment. She was tired, scared, and at the end of her rope. She closed her eyes and buried her face in his sturdy shoulder. Cool cotton pressed against the warm skin of her cheek, and the tantalizing scent of Owen's cologne mixed with the lemony scent of fabric softener filled her nostrils. Warm hands lightly smoothed her back, granting her a moment of security. Maybe with Owen's help she would find her music. Owen was indeed a rare and impressive man. He had understood about the music. She buried her face deeper and sighed.

His fingers tightened on her back and into her hair as her wistful sigh ripped at his heart. She had been so brave coming to him and demanding her music back. He would gladly have given it to her, if only he knew how. Owen tenderly cupped her jaw and tilted up her face. His gaze settled on the liquid pools gathered in her eyes. A fleeting smile teased the corners of his mouth as an idea came to him. "Are you positive my kiss took the music?"

"Positive? Not really, but it's the only thing I could come up with." She leaned away from the comfort of Owen's chest and swiped the back of her hand over her eyes. "Why?"

His teasing smile turned a little more rakish. "Suppose I kiss you again. Do you think the music will return?"

She pushed against his chest with her hands. "How would I know?" Owen's embrace tightened. "I didn't even know that a kiss would steal it."

"We could try again."

Nadia glanced wildly around the room. "Try what again?"

"A kiss." He kept his one arm around her and gently captured her chin with his other hand. "One simple kiss, Nadia, that's all." His thumb stroked the fullness of her lower lip. "What could it harm?"

Was he crazy? His first kiss had stolen her music; this one just might steal her soul. "I don't know, Owen. It could be dangerous." Huge, dark eyes stared up and begged him to understand.

"Dangerous? Maybe." He knew exactly what another kiss could be dangerous to: his sanity. The taste of Nadia five days ago had been slowly torturing him as he lay in his lonely bed night after night. "But if a kiss could take the music, it might also bring it back." His gaze settled on her mouth. "True?"

Nadia swallowed and ran the tip of her tongue over her suddenly dry lips. Maybe he was right. She stared at the sensual fullness of Owen's lower lip and wondered if it indeed tasted as intoxicating as she remembered. She softly parted her mouth and breathed. "Maybe."

Owen took her breathless word as permission and lowered his head. He didn't tighten his embrace as he softly slanted his mouth over hers. The kiss was as light and sweet as a summer's breeze, and just as fleeting. He raised his head and asked, "Hear anything yet?"

Nadia circled her arms around his neck and raised her mouth to his. "That wasn't how you kissed me the other night." She tugged his head lower until she could reach his lips. "Try it again."

Owen didn't need to be asked twice. His mouth slanted down on hers with all the pent-up hunger and frustration of the past days. His arms tightened like steel bans, crushing her to his chest. Need, like nothing he had ever experienced before, exploded low and hot within his body. He leaned farther back against the desk and spread his legs slightly so that she fitted snugly into the juncture of his thighs, where his desire was in full evidence.

His tongue slowly traced the voluptuous fullness of her lower lip, silently begging for entrance. When she softly sighed and parted her lips, he groaned deeply and thrust his tongue into her sweetness. The enticing riposte of her tongue charged the kiss with new life. This was not just *his* kiss. This was *their* kiss. Each was feeding off the other's hunger and desires.

He felt the gentle trembling of her fingers as she stroked his jaw and pressed herself closer. He was drowning in desire and the heavenly scent of Nadia. She smelled of fresh mountain air, sunshine, and a myriad of different wildflowers. The fingers of one hand twisted their way through curls of near-black silk, while his other hand cupped her hip and pressed her against the rigid bulge behind his jeans. He thought he would die when her hand traveled from his jaw to his knee and slowly climbed up to the top of his thigh.

He broke the kiss, tucked her head beneath his chin, and gasped for air. "If you want to keep this to just a kiss, don't move that hand another inch." He squinted up at the ceiling and prayed for strength. He could detect a slight trembling in her fingers, but they didn't climb higher.

He loosened his embrace and consoled himself that Nadia had responded to his kiss like gasoline to fire. He glanced down at the top of her head and softly asked, "Do you hear anything now?" He himself had heard fireworks, volcanoes exploding, comets whirling by, and a shifting of the earth's plates. She should be hearing the Mormon Tabernacle Choir by now.

Nadia slowly removed her hand and backed away from Owen. Her gaze never left his chest. She could still hear the pounding of his heart, the distant song of a bird somewhere outside, and the rushing surge of her blood crashing through her head with each beat of her heart. But no music. The kiss hadn't worked. She closed her eyes and shook her head. "Nothing."

Owen's heart lurched in his chest. He reached out and pulled her back into his arms. He held her close and whispered, "I'm willing to try again." He smiled when he felt her shoulders shake with silent laughter, and he knew that somehow they would get through this. "Hell, I'm willing to try all night if need be."

He was rewarded for his great sacrifice with an elbow in his gut and Nadia's sweet laughter. "You're rotten." She pushed a wayward curl out of her eye and chuckled. "And here I thought you were a gentleman."

He raised both hands in surrender. "I *am* a gentleman. If you don't believe me, just ask my aunt. She'll tell you."

Nadia busied herself with tucking in her red-and-white-striped top that had somehow managed to escape the waistband of her shorts. How had she allowed things to get so far out of hand? It was only supposed to be a kiss. "Your aunt is probably prejudiced." She smoothed out a wrinkle from her shorts. "Blood and water, and all that stuff."

Owen chuckled. "The saying is 'Blood is thicker than water.' " He raised one eyebrow and winked. "But I was brought up to be a proper gentleman, and you would be amazed to what lengths I would go for a woman in distress."

Nadia's gaze shot to the front of his straining jeans. She could see the length he was willing to go to on her account. A very impressive-looking length.

Heat flared into her cheeks as she heard Owen suck in his breath. Her gaze shot up, and she flushed redder when she encountered the obvious hunger burning in his gaze. She quickly glanced away. "Maybe this wasn't such a good idea."

Owen slowly shook his head. "It was an excellent idea." He pushed himself away and moved to stand behind the desk. "I think we may be onto something here."

She cocked an eyebrow and placed her hands on her hips. "And I think all the blood has drained from your brain."

His rich laughter filled the room. "I don't think so, Nadia." He glanced down to the front of his jeans and grinned rakishly. "I know so."

"I thought you said you were a gentleman?"

"I wasn't the one to bring it up."

Nadia flushed with guilt and looked away. "I'm sorry about that." She pushed the toe of the sneaker against the thick beige carpet and watched as the texture changed. "I didn't mean for things to get so out of control."

Owen bit his lip to keep from laughing again. "I was referring to bringing *it* up in the conversation, Nadia." He sat down and tried to look relaxed. "What I meant was, since I was there when the music stopped, wouldn't it seem logical that I would have to be there when the music starts back up?"

"Nothing about this is logical, Owen." She stepped back over to the doors and frowned at the perfectly green manicured lawn. "How many women in your life ever accused you of kissing the music straight out of their heads?"

"I have to admit, Nadia, you're the first." He leaned back into the chair and folded his arms behind his head.

"How many musicians have you kissed?" Maybe it was some type of electrical impulse or something.

"I think you're the first." He squinted up at the ceiling. "No, wait. I kissed Susie Reynolds in the seventh grade, and she used to play the piano."

"Could she still play after you kissed her?"

"Afraid so." He propped his feet up on the edge of the desk, gazing at Nadia being drenched by sunlight pouring in through the doors. "When exactly did you notice the music was gone?"

"When I went inside the house and closed the door."

"When did you last hear the music?"

"While standing on the porch." She remembered the turbulent cadenza raging through her head when she'd told Owen she couldn't see him again. Her emotions and her common sense had been competing to see which could screech the loudest.

"That just proves my point."

"What point?" She turned back toward Owen.

"I'm the missing factor." He lowered his feet and stood up. "Somehow I'm involved in your music vanishing."

"But the kiss didn't work."

"Maybe we didn't do it right." He chuckled at the look of astonishment clouding her face. "What I mean is, maybe we have to kiss on the porch again. Or maybe it has to be at the same time, or maybe it has to be on a full stomach."

"Or maybe it wasn't the kiss at all," said Nadia softly. She turned away before he could notice the tears filling up her eyes again. Coming here had been a mistake.

Owen came up behind her and gently touched her arm. "You may be right. Maybe it wasn't the kiss, Nadia, but there has to be a reason somewhere." His fingers caressed the smooth skin from her wrist to her elbow. "I'm willing to help you find it."

"How?"

"I don't know how. That's something we are going to have to work on together." He tenderly stroked the dark circles under her eyes. "The first thing you have to do is rest more. This obviously has you very upset, and I can sympathize with you on that, but you need your sleep."

"I need my music more." She didn't need to be told she looked like hell. She had a mirror at home. She knew exactly what she looked like.

"No, you need to relax. Maybe the music is trying to come back and you're too wound up to notice." His hands gently brushed her hair aside and massaged the tense muscles in her neck. "Have you ever been to Hidden Valley?"

She tilted her head forward and sighed as Owen's warm fingers worked their magic, easing the pressure from her neck and shoulders. "As in the salad dressing?"

"No." Owen chuckled. "Hidden Valley is a secluded valley about ten miles out of town. Not many people know about it, and the ones who do keep it to themselves. It's a small piece of paradise with gurgling streams, a small waterfall, and acres of blue skies and green grass."

"It sounds lovely."

"Great." He gave a final squeeze to her neck. "I'll go fix a picnic basket, and we'll be on our way."

"Wait a minute." Nadia quickly turned around and frowned. "I didn't say I was going anywhere." She didn't like the determined gleam in Owen's eyes. "I have things to do back at the ranch."

"What do you have to do that is more important than getting back your music?"

Nadia worried her lower lip with her teeth. "If I go with you to this Hidden Valley, who is to say the music will return?"

"Who's to say it won't?"

She was torn. Was there a possibility that the music would return if she went on a picnic with Owen to this hidden paradise? Could she afford not to go? She had vowed to put a great deal of distance between Owen and herself. He was too tempting, but now, with the disappearance of her music, could she risk *not* seeing him? What would happen if he was right, and the music would only return with his help? Surely she had enough control to keep her heart safe for one afternoon by keeping their relationship on some level of friendship. "If I go, it would be out of friendship, nothing more."

Owen nodded his head and smiled. He got the message. "I only have one question?"

"What's that?"

"Do you prefer fried chicken or bologna sandwiches?"

Nadia glanced at the other two cars parked at the side of the road and took the quilt Owen handed her. "I thought you said only a few people knew about this place."

Owen picked up the heavy wicker picnic basket and shut the hood of the trunk. He glanced at the two other cars. "Don't worry, we probably won't even run into them. There's more than a hundred acres of woods and meadows."

"I have more than that on the ranch, and every time I turn around, there's always someone there."

He chuckled and led the way to a dirt path hidden between two massive pine trees. "I can imagine."

Nadia ducked beneath a low-hanging branch and glanced around for NO TRESPASSING signs. There weren't any. "Who owns all this?"

"We do." He held a branch back so that she could pass.

"We do?"

"You're a taxpayer, aren't you?"

"At times more than I care to be." She looked around her with interest. The forest was thick with massive trees and the sweet smell of peat. The path Owen was following was nonexistent, and the air was a good ten degrees cooler and still damp from the previous night's late thundershower. "The government owns all this?"

"They bought it back in the seventies and earmarked it for a park." He held her hand and helped her step over a fallen log. "It's our good fortune that they haven't come up with the funds yet to knock down half an acre of trees to blacktop a massive parking lot, asphalt a couple of miles of trails, or throw up dozens of picnic tables." He grinned, and waved an arm toward a patch of sunlight streaming through the thick trees ahead of them. "In other words it's still as nature intended it to be—natural."

Nadia stepped into the clearing and stared in awe at the beauty surrounding her. The valley was spread out below them, and the mountains were above them. The path Owen had been following had brought them straight into paradise.

"What do you think? Can you relax here?"

She had never missed her music as much as at this moment. The melody this valley could inspire would surely rival anything Brahms or Liszt ever wrote. "*Beautiful* doesn't begin to do it justice."

He reached for her hand and gently squeezed it. "My sentiments exactly." He started to pull her through some tall grass and toward another clump of trees. "Come on. The best spot for a picnic is on the other side of the valley."

Nadia rolled onto her back and groaned. "I can't believe all that food you packed. Who were you expecting, sumo-wrestling park rangers?"

"I didn't see you complaining five minutes ago when I pulled out those two thick slices of chocolate cake." He chuckled as he finished packing away the remaining food and pushed the basket out of the way. Nadia looked so relaxed with her face raised to the sun and her bare toes wiggling in the soft grass at the foot of the quilt. The picnic had been a stroke of brilliance on his part. Not only was he getting to share some time with Nadia, but the shadows that had to be haunting her in his office had disappeared. He wasn't sure if he wanted the music to return—she might start in again about how they weren't right for each other.

He wasn't claiming that it was Nadia who was to make Aunt Verna ecstatically happy and start pulling out the family Bible to add another name to the frail pages. But he wasn't going to discount the possibility either. He was thirty-three years old, and he recognized a good thing when he saw it. The physical attraction between Nadia and himself would be downright frightening if it weren't so exciting. She was intelligent, caring, loving, and unbelievably sexy. He owed it to himself, as well as to her, to push this relationship as far as it could go. As his aunt Verna was so fond of reminding him, he wasn't getting any younger. If he wanted to have those six kids he always dreamed about, he'd better start thinking marriage.

He turned his head and glanced over at Nadia. She was turned onto her side with her arm under her head as a pillow. Her eyes, which could dance with laughter or burn with desire, were halfway closed, and a sleepy smile played across her mouth. She was studying him. He reached into his pocket and placed a coin on the blanket between them. "Penny for your thoughts."

She smiled at the copper coin. "Is that all they're worth?"

"It depends on what they're about." He teasingly jingled the coins in his pockets.

"I was thinking of you." She placed a hand over her mouth and tried to smother a yawn. The sun was dissolving all the tension in her body with its warmth. She felt as if she were melting into the quilt.

"Ah." He placed another coin next to the penny. "Will this cover it, then?"

She chuckled softly at the shiny dime and pressed her cheek farther into her arm. "That's about right." She closed her eyes as contentment settled over her. "I was wondering why some woman hadn't pinched you up by now."

"Pinched me up by now?"

"You know—brought you to the altar, followed by two-point-three children, a dog, and an orthodontist bill."

"The saying is 'snapped me up,' not 'pinched me up.'" He pulled a long blade of grass and idly twirled it around his fingers. "So you think I'll make a great catch?"

"Trout make a great catch. You would make a great husband." She stifled another yawn. "So why aren't you married?"

He gazed at her. She looked partially asleep, all soft and cuddly. "The right woman never tried to snap me up."

"Hmmm . . ." She nodded her head somewhat, closed her eyes, and mumbled, "Maybe she should have tried to pinch you instead."

Owen frowned. Here they were discussing the main topic of conversation in Crow's Head, his marital status, and Nadia had fallen asleep! Didn't she care that he was the most eligible bachelor in the western part of the state? Hell, it could be the entire state for all he knew, and the one woman he wouldn't mind answering a few questions for couldn't even bother to ask them.

He reached over and tenderly brushed a curl off her face, then tucked it behind her ear. She looked like an angel, all soft and heavenly. Thick, dark lashes were fanned out against her cheeks, and her lips were softly parted. He could detect a small smile playing at the corner of her mouth, and he wondered what she was thinking.

Stretching out beside her, he watched, entranced, as the sunlight played across her face. He wondered what it would be like to wake up next to this woman night after night, year after year.

FIVE

Nadia wiggled her nose and brushed her hand across her face. Something was disturbing her sleep, and she wanted it to stop. When the irritating insect tickled her nose again, she stuck out her lower lip and blew. Her eyes flew open as a deep chuckle sounded next to her ear. Rich brown eyes, the color of thick, creamy chocolate stared back at her. Owen's eyes. She'd know them anywhere.

She smothered a yawn and glanced around. The sun had moved halfway across the heavens. "Oh, my! Why didn't you wake me?" She quickly sat up and gazed down at the man still stretched out on the quilt. He looked as if he didn't have a care in the world.

"Do you know you talk in your sleep?"

"I do not!" She ran her fingers through her hair and tugged at her shirt. A frown pulled at the smooth skin of her brow as she studied his relaxed expression. "Do I really?"

"Uh-hmmm . . ." He idly twirled the piece of long

grass he had used to tickle her nose between his fingers.

"What did I say?" He looked as if he knew a secret. Was she reading more into his expression than was there?

"I couldn't understand most of it." His lips twitched with some hidden amusement.

"I was mumbling?" She tried to remember what she had been dreaming about and came up with a blank. It could have been anything, or everything.

He frowned at the blade of grass for a moment before looking up at her. "No, you weren't mumbling." A devilish grin lit up his face. "You were speaking in some foreign language."

"Russian?" He shook his head. "German?"

"No."

"Polish? Czech? Slovak?"

Owen stared at her in awe. "How many languages do you speak?"

"Fluently?"

He raised his gaze toward the heavens. "I'll bite, fluently."

"You bite what?"

He chuckled and bit back his response. Nadia didn't seem ready to listen to what he would like to nibble on. "It's a saying, like 'I give.'"

She frowned momentarily at the slang. English was the hardest language she had ever learned, and she still had her doubts about ever attaining perfect fluency. "Counting English, I speak eight different languages."

Owen whistled softly. "What university did you attend?" He'd had four years of Spanish, between high school and college, and had promptly forgotten it all. Crow's Head, North Carolina, wasn't the hub of cultural diversity.

"I didn't attend any university." She didn't like the gleam of admiration she had noticed in Owen's gaze. There was absolutely nothing special or remarkable about her education. "I just earned my GED two years ago in New York, and I haven't found the time to sign up for any college courses yet."

Owen's mouth dropped open in astonishment. "Where did you learn so many languages, then?"

"When you're living in Russia, it pays to speak Russian."

"You lived in Russia?" He never met anyone who'd lived in Russia before.

"And Poland, Czechoslovakia, Hungary, Austria, Germany, Yugoslavia, Bulgaria—just to name a few."

"A few!"

"My family believes in being well traveled." She shrugged her shoulders. "When someone asks me where I grew up, I just reply, 'Europe.' It's easier than naming all the different countries."

"But where was your home?"

"The *vardo* was my home—we took it with us everywhere we went." She reached over and picked a fat cloverleaf. Today wasn't her lucky day; it had only three leaves. "We are the Romany people—Gypsies, Owen, not your average American family."

"So what made you leave Europe and come to America?"

"The fighting." She gazed off into the distance and stared at the peaceful mountaintops and fluffy white clouds dotting the brilliant blue skies. "I was sick of the wars. Everywhere we went, it was the same. People wanting to overthrow their government, killing each other in the name of religion, and countries splitting into smaller countries and calling it democracy." A shiver shook her slender body, and she hugged herself as tears filled her eyes. "It became a very dangerous place to live for a family that wouldn't choose sides. They figured if you weren't for them, you were against them. All we wanted was to be left in peace."

Owen sat up and moved closer to her. Lord, what she must have seen and lived through in her young life. He placed his arm around her shoulder and gently drew her toward him. "You're safe here."

She leaned into his warmth and closed her eyes against the memories and fear. The memories of her first twenty-three years of life living in Europe, and the fear from the four and a half years she'd worried about her family still there. It had taken her that long to get them all out. They had refused to come to America unless they all came together. So for more than four years she'd worried, never knowing half the time even what country they were in. The sporadic phone calls came all too infrequently, and CNN became more of a curse, with its hot-spot journalism and up-to-the-minute reporting, than a help. Europe had had so many hot spots in the last four years that they should have just called it Hades and been done with it.

"Why did you pick America instead of some other country, such as Canada, or Scotland even?"

"Because it's a place you could feel homesick about." She turned her head and glanced up at him. "When I was eight, I attended a school in West Germany for about six months. The teacher was an American married to some military officer stationed over there. She used to tell such wonderful stories about Toledo, Ohio, that I knew she was homesick for America." She smiled self-consciously. "I guess I made up my mind right then and there that I would be going to the United States."

His warm palm cupped her cheek, and his smile grew. "I guess I should be thankful that she wasn't from Paris or London." His hungry gaze fastened on her mouth.

A faint blush warmed her face, and her bottom lip trembled. "It would have been cheaper if she had been." They were heading back onto dangerous ground, one she was bound and determined to avoid. She pulled away from the tempting heat of his body and glanced at the breathtaking beauty surrounding them. Owen had been right. They hadn't seen any signs of the occupants of the other two cars. "Where is this waterfall that you promised me?" She remembered crossing a crude, makeshift bridge made from a couple of logs, but no waterfall.

"We'll go that way back to the car if you're up to it." He glanced down at the creamy smoothness of her shapely legs. Legs that were better suited for being wrapped around his hips than to be hiking through the woods.

"What do you mean, 'if I'm up to it'?"

"We have to hike up the side of that mountain." He nodded his head eastward.

She looked offended that he should even doubt that she could make it. "That, my dear *friend*, is a hill, not a mountain."

"It's part of the Smoky Mountains, so it's a mountain."

She give an unladylike snort and reached for her sneakers. They weren't the most practical shoes for trekking through the woods, but when she'd gone to Owen's house this morning, having a picnic had been the last thing on her mind. "If you have ever seen the Alps, that"—she jerked her head in the direction of the mountain—"wouldn't even classify as a hill."

An hour later Nadia had revised her thinking. Either this indeed was a mountain, or she was terribly out of shape. The back of her calves protested every step upward, and a fine sheen of perspiration made her clothes cling to her skin. But she would bite off her own tongue before asking how much farther.

Owen glanced behind him and shook his head with admiration. Either Nadia was the most stubborn woman he had ever met or beneath that delicate package of femininity beat the heart of a mountain goat. He had climbed this trail dozens of times, and each time he promised himself it would get easier. It never did. "It's not much farther."

She brushed a damp curl away from her forehead and forced herself to stop panting. If she stopped now, every muscle in her body would freeze, and she would never make it to the blasted waterfall. She forced herself to smile pleasantly.

Owen shifted the picnic basket to his other hand and continued to pick his way over fallen trees, around brush, and over the occasional exposed root. Maybe he shouldn't have been so chauvinistic and allowed Nadia to carry the quilt instead of folding it up and jamming it into the basket. She seemed to be holding up better than he was. He paused and listened for a moment. "I hear it."

"Hear what?" The only sound she heard was the rapid pounding of her heart, the agonizing screams of her muscles, and the occasional chirping of a bird.

"The waterfall." He grabbed her hand and hurried toward the sound. "Don't you hear it?"

Nadia was positive that she wouldn't have heard Niagara Falls even if she were standing under it. "I don't hear . . ." She followed Owen and ducked under a low-hanging branch. "Wait! I hear it." The crisp, clean sound of splashing water renewed her energy. They had made it! She gave a breathless laugh and quickened her pace.

Owen responded to Nadia's revitalized energy and pushed his way through a dense clump of mountain laurel. He stopped as soon as they cleared the bushes, and grinned at the sight in front of them. Hidden Valley Falls was as awe-inspiring as when he last saw it. Tons of water crashed down the fifty-foot drop into the shimmering pool below. Massive trees and shrubs clung to the rocks, and boulders on either side of the falls glittered with the spray of the thundering cascade. One end of the pool was foamy and turbulent under the pounding of the waterfall, but the rest was smooth as silk, cool, and inviting. Many were the times, after hiking all the way up here, that he had stripped down to his skivvies and dived straight into its inviting waters.

"How deep is it?"

He turned and looked at Nadia. She was standing on the bank of the pool, staring into it. He gauged the level of the water. "Around three to four feet at the edge, and it goes to about twelve feet in the middle."

"Rocks?"

"A couple stick out from under the falls, but the rest of the pool is clear." He moved up and stood beside her. He had never brought a woman up here before, but he'd expected her to gush about the beauty of the falls and the faint rainbow shimmering in the mist, not ask about rocks. He told her, "The bottom is made up of smooth rocks and stones, and there might be a couple of fish swimming in there." He frowned as Nadia dug through the pockets of her shorts and handed him a pack of gum.

"Could you hold that for a moment, please?"

Owen glanced at the green pack of gum resting in the palm of his hand. "Why?" He looked back at Nadia just as she dived off the bank and into the pool. He glanced back down at the pack of gum and noticed Nadia's sneakers sitting forlornly on the bank. He hadn't even noticed when she had kicked them off.

He glanced back at the pool and frowned. Where was she? She should have surfaced by now. Lord, he didn't even know if she could swim. He stared at the surface of the pool and dropped the picnic basket and her gum. Just because she could execute a perfect dive into the water didn't mean she knew how to swim. What if a boulder had made its way to the bottom of the pool since the last time he had swum there? She could have whacked her head and been in the process of drowning, right this minute.

He was in the process of yanking off his sneakers when her head broke the water on the other side of the pool. Her grin flashed with all the brilliance of a diamond. "You forgot to tell me how cold it is," she yelled over the thundering of the falls.

"Serves you right." He dropped his sneakers next to hers. "You shouldn't have dived in like that."

"Why not?"

"Because it might not have been safe."

She laughed and brushed her wet hair away from her face. "You're the one who told me there weren't any rocks." She pushed away from the rocky bottom and floated on her back. "I'm sorry, Owen, I just couldn't wait. It's been years since I swam with nature." She lightly kicked her feet and raised her face toward the sun. "Maybe I could widen a section of the stream that goes through the ranch and make a swimming hole out of it."

"Wouldn't it be easier to buy a pool?" He stared at her top, which was clinging to her breasts, and swallowed hard. She was fully clothed and was still the most exotic sight he had ever seen. His gaze slid down until it encountered cute pink toes sticking above the shimmering water.

"Why would I want to swim in a bunch of chemicals? The chlorine dries out my skin and makes my eyes burn."

"You prefer swimming with fish?" He'd always had a feeling Nadia was different from any other woman he'd dated; now he knew it.

"Any day." She flipped over and dived back under the water. She surfaced a minute later holding a tiny pebble in her hand. She brushed the hair out of her eyes and studied the stone. It was deep green with threads of black weaving their way through it. She swam over to Owen and handed him the pebble. "Could you please put this with my gum."

"Souvenir?"

"Nope." She pulled her top away from her chest, only to have it suck right back to it when she released the material. "One of my cousins has a rock collection." She frowned at sweat clinging to his hair. "Aren't you coming in?"

"You might be able to swim in those shorts and top, but I'm afraid these jeans weren't made for swimming."

Nadia shrugged her shoulders and swam back to the middle of the pond. "Take them off." He had to be as hot as she was after climbing up the side of the mountain. It seemed highly unfair that she could cool off while for the sake of her modesty he had to bake in his own sweat. Who was she to stand in the way of Owen swimming? She could handle him splashing around in his underwear, providing there was at least thirty feet of chilly water between them and she kept her mind on other things, such as glaciers.

Owen choked on his next breath. Was she serious? "You wouldn't mind me swimming around buck naked?" Maybe he misjudged her definition of friendship.

Nadia stopped swimming and treaded water for a moment. Her eyes narrowed as she slowly ran her gaze down his body. She would bet the deed to the ranch he had underwear on under those jeans. No self-respecting southern gentleman would be caught dead without them. She smiled nonchalantly. "I'm sure you don't have anything I haven't seen before." Owen raised an eyebrow at that comment, and her smile widened. "I happen to have four brothers."

His lips twitched with amusement. "So you wouldn't mind?" He never swam here buck naked before, but there was a first time for everything. He glanced at the deep pool and wondered what else might be swimming in there besides Nadia. If the family jewels were going on display, he wanted to know how much danger they were going to be in. He didn't need some ravenous snapper turtle taking a bite out of the future generation of Prescotts.

"Not in the least." She took another stroke, stopped, and glanced back up at Owen. "The fish might not be so generous." She smiled wickedly. "You'd be surprised what they nibble on when they're hungry."

Owen's fingers froze on the snap of his jeans. She must have been reading his mind. "Are there witches in Russia?" A rueful grin teased his mouth.

"Witches?" Nadia floated for a moment and chuckled softly. "If you believe their folk tales, then yes, there are many witches in Russia."

He pulled his shirt up over his head and dropped it to the ground next to his sneakers. "I believe they became one short on the day you came to America."

Nadia held his gaze until curiosity got the better of her, and she lowered it to his chest. His shoulders went on forever, soft, downy curls arched across his chest, inviting a lover's touch, and his stomach looked rock-hard. Worn denim jeans were slung low on his hips, enticing her gaze to follow the contrast between deep-blue material and the bronze smoothness of his skin. Her gaze jerked upward when his deft fingers unsnapped the waistband. "In Europe it isn't a compliment to call someone a witch." She remembered some local villagers taunting her and her sisters with hateful, nasty names during their youth. "Witch" was always one of the names they hurled, along with "thief" and "beggar." If it was a good day, stones and sticks weren't thrown after the insults.

"In America it all depends on how you mean it." He stepped out of his jeans and pulled off his socks.

"How do you mean it?" Her gaze was fastened onto his face. She didn't look to see if he had indeed left on his underwear.

"You read my mind just a minute ago." He neatly folded his socks and placed them on top of his jeans.

"Many people have accused my aunt Sasha of mind reading, but she swears she sees what people show with their eyes and the way their bodies talk." She glanced down at Owen's body, wondering what it would say to her. Navy-blue-and-white-striped boxer shorts said he had indeed respected her modesty. "No one has ever accused me of mind reading before."

"Maybe you can't read my mind. Maybe we both just think on the same wavelength." With a graceful dive he entered the pond with barely a splash. He surfaced two feet in front of her and shook his head, sending a shower of droplets spraying in all directions. "But you are still a witch."

"Why?" She didn't like that word. It was a hateful word that provoked too many memories.

He tenderly reached out and traced a drop of moisture slowing rolling down her cheek. "I think you've cast a spell over me." His finger stroked the fullness of her lower lip. "A bewitching"—he moved closer and his leg gently bumped against hers—"enchanting"—his breath feathered across her trembling mouth—"charming spell." His words ended with a sweet kiss.

Nadia melted under his tender assault and forgot to keep treading water. They both went under with their lips sealed and came up sputtering and gasping for breath a full minute later. Her eyes sparkled with laughter as she kicked away from Owen and splashed him with a spray of water. "You're dangerous!" They both could have drowned.

Owen grinned back and wiped the water from his face. "You're delicious."

"I thought I was a witch?"

"You're a delicious witch." He allowed the distance between them to grow. Thousands of gallons of chilly creek water were rapidly turning into a hot spring. This wasn't the time or the place to prove to Nadia how great they could be together. She had come along under the terms of friendship, and what he wanted to do was not in that category. Not only were they in a public place, where anyone could happen along at any time, but it was physically impossible to make love to a woman while swimming in a twelve-foot-deep pond. Not that he wasn't willing to try. It ranked higher on his list of ways to meet your Maker than hanging, but it still wasn't his number-one choice.

He glanced over at Nadia. "Last one to reach that boulder"—he pointed to a huge rock embedded in the bank of the other side of the pool—"has to carry the picnic basket back to the car."

Nadia looked over her shoulder at the boulder and then back at Owen. "Ready, set, go!" She flipped over and started to swim in one fluid motion. She had a three-stroke lead before the startled Owen even began his hopeless attempt to catch up.

Nadia glanced through the windshield as Owen's car slowly made its way up her rutted drive. On the way to Hidden Valley they had dropped off her car so that she wouldn't have to backtrack from Owen's. She distinctly remembered parking it by the house; now it was parked by the barn, and someone had turned on her porch light. She hoped it was her father or one of her uncles who had borrowed the car. Her brothers tended to collect tickets the way little Damek collected his rocks. She had spent the entire day, and a good portion of the evening, with Owen. There was no telling what kind of trouble her family had gotten into.

On the way home from Hidden Valley she had refused to go inside a restaurant wearing clothes that looked as if she'd slept in them. Her shorts and top were dry, pretty much on the clean side, but the wrinkles were terminal. Owen had gotten his way and bought her dinner when he found a roadside diner with secluded picnic tables; fat, juicy hamburgers; and the crispest fries she had ever tasted. For two hours they wolfed down their meal, fought off killer mosquitoes, and laughed. She had a wonderful time trading childhood stories with Owen. Not only was he the sole child of the town's most influential and wealthy family, but he had a curious mind and had gotten into more scrapes than all her brothers combined. It seemed that money, prestige, and power only gave Owen an added edge on his adventurous nature.

Night had gently fallen during their meal, cloaking them in a seductive darkness. She had been reluctant to leave their private haven, but she knew it couldn't last. The wonderful day with Owen had to end. Reality and home were calling. She glanced at her house. Only the porch light radiated a warm glow of welcome, but it stopped at the front door. The house itself was dark and lonely. Since when did it bother her to come home to an empty house?

Owen parked the car and glanced around the yard. "Everyone must be at the camp." He glanced at the house sitting all alone. "Why are you the only one who lives in the house?"

"The rest prefer the camp and the old way of life." She climbed out of the car and started for the porch.

Owen followed her up the two steps. "Don't you like the old way?"

"I have nothing against the simple life." She walked

over to the railing and stared out toward the hills where the camp lay. "But I also have nothing against a bathroom down the hall, running water, and electricity."

"Your family has all that." He leaned against a post and studied the gentle curve of her cheek, the way her hair had dried into a wild mass of untamed curls, and the provocative fullness of her lower lip. "You could live in one of those mobile homes at the camp."

"What's wrong with me living in the perfectly good house that came with the ranch?"

"You're not with your family." From everything he knew about Nadia, her family was very important to her. They ranked right up there with her music.

"My family is no more than a quarter of a mile over that hill." Her head nodded in the direction she had been staring.

"So why aren't you with them?"

"I'm perfectly content living here alone."

"But are you happy?"

She crossed her arms over her chest and snapped, "What's that supposed to mean?"

Owen picked up the strain in her voice and decided to back off for now. For some reason Nadia always held herself a little bit apart from her otherwise close-knit family. "Sometimes when I look into your eyes, I see a great sadness." *And secrets. Dangerous secrets you try to hide from everyone.*

Nadia's teeth worried her lower lip. "You must be mistaken. I have everything I always wanted. My family is well, nearby, and living in a war-free country.

I own, or will own in twenty years, one of the greatest horse-breeding ranches in North Carolina. I am beginning on a fabulous and possibly highly profitable career. The only thing I'm missing is my music, and as soon as I get it back, my life will be complete."

He took a step closer. "But what about you, Nadia?"

"What about me?" She took a step back and ended up with her back against a post.

"Are you happy?" He moved nearer and tenderly cupped her cheek.

"Why shouldn't I be?" Her voice shook, but she kept her chin up and held her ground.

His hungry gaze fastened on her mouth. He leaned in closer and lowered his head. "You tell me, Nadia." His breath teased the corner of her mouth as his tongue faintly outlined her passion-swollen lower lip. "Tell me what would make you happy." He sighed into her mouth as she slowly parted her lips and yielded to his gentle onslaught.

Owen felt her arms encircle his neck and her breasts crush against his chest. He plunged his tongue into her mouth and drank from her sweetness. Thoughts of making her happy vanished from his mind. He wanted her hot, wild, and as hungry for him as he was for her. He wanted to carry her through her empty little house, up the stairs, place her down on her bed, and make sweet, hot love to her till the ache she had caused inside him eased. His hand stroked the enticing flare of her hip and caressed the tempting roundness of her bottom. He pulled her in closer and pressed her abdomen against his straining manhood. He figured it would take at least sixty years for the ache to ease so that he could start to breathe normally around her.

"Nadia!" He groaned her name in need as he broke the kiss. He loosened his hold and blazed a trail of kisses over her jaw, down her throat, to the rapidly pounding pulse thundering in the side of her neck. His teeth sank into the pulse with a teasing playfulness before climbing up to capture a dainty lobe. He toyed with a golden hoop earring, sending it gently swinging with his breath. "Tell me what would make you happy."

Nadia closed her eyes and said a silent prayer in Russian. One that would hopefully grant her courage, wisdom, and the strength to go against what her body was begging for—release. To take Owen into her home and into her bed would be taking him into her heart and risking the greatest sorrow of her life. She had been so strong for so long for so many people, she didn't know if she had anything left for herself. Her life was centered around her family and her music. There wasn't time or energy left over for anything else. Maybe once the album was finished, she could get out more and possibly start to date. Owen was the wrong man for her, no matter what her body said.

With a heavy sigh she leaned back against the post for support and gave the only answer she could. "Having my music return would make me happy."

SIX

Owen stood in the shadows of the barn and watched in awe as Nadia wove her magic. He had been right earlier; she was indeed a witch. Her sweet, gentle voice was low and throaty, and her fingers moved as gracefully as the wind over the strings of her acoustic guitar. He had no idea what language she was singing, or even what the words were, but with her song she was seducing the hell out of him. The amazing part was, she had no idea that she was doing it. She hadn't even noticed when he had entered the barn ten minutes ago. At first he had thought her music had returned, but he now realized she was singing the same song over and over again, although in different languages, and she was reading sheet music that was spread out in front of her on the hay.

He glanced at IRS, who was standing motionless in his stall gazing at Nadia. He wondered if it was possible for a horse to feel longing, or was he being fanciful and misinterpreting the look in IRS's soulful brown eyes? Whatever it was, Owen understood exactly how IRS felt. Nadia was a vision sitting in the sweet-smelling hay wearing nothing but a skimpy pair of denim shorts and a sleeveless red-and-white-checked blouse. She had twisted a red bandanna and made it into a headband to keep the wild curls away from her face. He smiled as she stopped for a moment, worried her lower lip, and then quickly scribbled something on the page in front of her.

When she resumed her singing, he closed his eyes and allowed the music to wash over him. He knew she was working on a children's album about animals, but the foreign words gave the light little number a very provocative sound. He silently cursed and shifted his weight when he felt his jeans become a little too snug. Nadia seemed to have that effect on him, no matter what she was doing.

Last night when she had said that only the return of her music would make her happy, he felt she had been holding back something, and the secrets in her eyes had grown. She had wanted him as much as he wanted her. He had felt it in the way she melted in his arms, the way she flared up when he kissed her, but more important he had heard it in the heartfelt sigh that had escaped her when he had ended the kiss. For some reason Nadia had hid behind her music. He had left her standing on the porch with the promise that he would help her get back the music and a silent prayer that he would capture her heart in doing so. It hadn't come as a great shock to him that on the way home he realized Nadia had come to mean more to him than just a beautiful woman with an incredible body. He wanted to be the key to her happiness. He was falling in love. He wanted to be her knight in shining armor and return her music, then sweep her off her feet and into his bed. It was hell being a romantic southern gentleman with raging hormones. He took a deep breath, prayed that his physical condition wasn't too obvious, and stepped out of the shadows.

Nadia caught a movement out of the corner of her eye and glanced over to the far side of the barn. Her fingers stilled on the steel strings, and her voice faded away as he stepped into the light. "Owen?"

"I went to the house first, but no one was there."

"IRS likes to listen to me sing." She straightened up the scattered music and neatly placed it in a blue folder. "I thought maybe a change of scenery would inspire me."

"Did it?"

She glanced around in frustration at the mounds of hay, weathered planking, and the way the sunlight played with the dust particles as it streamed in through the huge open doors. She sadly shook her head and whispered, "No."

Owen sat down beside her in the hay. Her one-word answer told him so much. She was disappointed and didn't know what to try next. "Was the song you were singing one of the ones for the album?"

"Yes. I was just putting some final touches to it."

"How many songs have you written?"

"Twenty-three."

Owen glanced at her in surprise. "Surely that's enough to finish the album."

"No, I need one more." She plucked at a guitar string and sent a soulful note heavenward. "Children's albums are different from adults'. Some of my songs are short and simple, so the children can learn them quickly and sing along with the record. Others are more complex: They tell a story, and there's no constant chorus for the children to memorize. The song I'm missing is one of the complex ones."

"How long does it take you to write a song?"

"I've been working on the album for over two years now." She glanced down at the blue folder and all the translated copies of "Fearless Benny", a song about an ostrich named Benny who refused to hide his head in the sand. "I had half of it done when I signed the contract, and I've been working on it full-time ever since."

"And all you need is one more song?" It didn't sound totally impossible to him. How hard could it be to write one children's song after already writing twenty-three?

"Don't sound so hopeful." She laid the guitar aside and leaned back into the soft hay. "It's not as easy as it sounds."

"You can do it. I have all the faith in the world in you."

"Thank you for the vote of confidence, but you

seem to be forgetting that I'm missing the main ingredient of any song, the music."

"Improvise." He plucked a piece of straw from her hair and tickled her nose.

She chuckled and shook her head. "It would be like you trying to build a house without any wood." She brushed a piece of hay off his jeans. "Speaking of your work, why aren't you there?"

"I'm the boss"—he reached over and drew a line up her bare thigh with the straw—"and I decided I deserved the rest of this beautiful afternoon off." The only reason he had left work early was because he hadn't been accomplishing anything there. All he had done all morning was think of Nadia, her hot, sweet kisses, and the fact that he was falling in love. He just had to see her.

She snatched the piece of straw away from Owen. "What did you do that was so wonderful?"

He plucked up another piece of straw and leaned in closer, playfully teasing the corner of her mouth with the hay. "It's not what I did that was so wonderful; it's what I'm going to do." His hungry gaze followed the dried stem as it slowly made its way over the dewy softness of her lower lip.

Her voice held a breathless catch. "What are you going to do?"

"I'm going to kiss you."

She studied his mouth with fascination. "Is it going to be wonderful?"

He bent over her and lowered his head until his

mouth just barely grazed hers. Looking deep into the dark pools of her eyes, he whispered, "You tell me."

She raised her arms around his neck and smiled against his hovering mouth. "I never try to prejudge something."

He pulled back a fraction of an inch. "Not even when you have experienced it before?"

"Well, there're kisses"—she lightly ran her tongue over the seductive fullness of his lower lip—"and then, there're kisses."

He nipped at her upper lip in retaliation. "You might have a point there." His mouth came down hungrily on hers.

Nadia surrendered to the desires that were battling her self-control. Why was she fighting against Owen's tender onslaught? He was everything she had ever looked for in a man, and more. If he wouldn't take seriously her warning that they were wrong for each other, then that was his problem, not hers. Her problem was going to be safeguarding her heart. Owen had the potential to steal his way into her heart and destroy it. Men like Owen wouldn't want the happily-ever-after life with a girl like her. She had burned her bridges back in New York, and now she had to pay the price.

With a moan of need she tightened her hold around his neck and deepened the kiss. She felt the violent trembling of Owen's body as he pressed against her, sending her deeper into the soft bed of hay. His tongue was firm and relentless as it sought out every dark recess in her mouth. She opened up to him like a flower to sunshine.

Owen rejoiced in her surrender and tenderly cupped her cheek. The satiny smoothness of her skin warmed his palm and his heart. With leisurely slowness he moved his hand downward, past her pounding pulse, over the faint swell of her collarbone, until he reached the soft curves of her breast. His fingers shook as they outlined the top button of her blouse.

Nadia couldn't stand the wait any longer. She stroked his back and hastily pulled his shirt from the waistband of his jeans. Her mouth rained quick little kisses down his jaw as her hands slid under the shirt and caressed his back. Heat scorched her fingertips as they explored all the hollows and the bulges that had so intrigued her yesterday during their swim. He felt more wonderful than she had imagined. He was warm, solid, and incredibly sexy.

With the haste of frustration she pulled out her hands and tugged at the buttons running down the front of his shirt. She wanted to run her fingers through the fine, dark hair covering his chest. She wanted to run her mouth over his fiery skin.

Owen stopped toying with the buttons on her blouse and helped her by ripping off his shirt and throwing it to the side. The prospects of having Nadia's hands all over him had blown what little control he had left.

Nadia reached up and drew a small, moist circle with her tongue over the pounding pulse throbbing in his neck. She felt the trembling of his body under her mouth and knew that Owen was about to go up in flames and she was holding the match. Her mouth slid down his chest, captured one of his hard, dark nipples, and playfully teased it with her teeth. The heat radiating from his body intensified.

Her hands stroked his shoulders, and her lips greedily tasted every inch of his chest. Her blood sang an aubade as it whirled through her body, waking up every nerve, every cell. It was the morning song, and it aroused portions of her body that had been asleep for a very long time. Too long. Her breasts surged against the frothy lace of her bra. She could feel the nipples harden and become sensitive against the material. The emptiness burning inside her was the worst. She wanted to feel Owen deep inside her, satisfying this horrible ache he had caused. Her fingers reached for the snap of his jeans as she moaned his name.

The tips of her fingers seared his stomach as they fumbled with the copper snap. His heart stopped beating when he heard voices and the sound of a truck pulling up outside the barn. He sucked in a ragged breath and groaned, "Please tell me that's not voices I hear."

Nadia closed her eyes and sighed. Of all the terrible timing . . . "It's my brothers and Uncle Rupa."

Owen rolled off of her and hurriedly reached for his shirt. "Are they coming in here?"

She sat up and brushed straw from her blouse and

shorts. A frown pulled at her mouth as she listened. "I would guess so." She glanced at Owen and marveled at the way he was tugging on his shirt and buttoning it. How could he possibly be thinking straight after what they had been doing? She hadn't even heard the truck pull up outside. "Unless you think they are taking that horse into my house."

"What horse?" He was jamming the ends of his shirt into his jeans when he heard a cry from a horse outside the barn. He glanced over at IRS, who was answering the distant cry.

"That's a very good question." Nadia stood up and brushed at the hay clinging to her clothes. She picked a few pieces out of her wild mane as she marched to the opened barn doors.

Owen quickly ran his fingers through his hair, double-checked his appearance, and hurried after her. He hadn't liked the look on her face; it was the same one she had worn when she confronted him about losing her music. Someone was in for a world of trouble, but for once it was not he.

Nadia stepped out into the sunlight as the door to a horse trailer was slammed shut. She watched as a tall, lanky man climbed back into the cab of the truck and drove away. By the speed at which the truck was taking her rutted and perilous driveway, she would guess the driver wasn't in the best of moods. Well, tough goulash, neither was she.

She turned and stared at the beautiful mare, fenced in the corral, who was curiously inspecting her surroundings. She appeared healthy, well taken care of, and expensive. Nadia glared at her uncle and her two brothers, who were proudly leaning against the fencing admiring the mare and congratulating themselves. "Are we taking in boarders now?"

Rupa laughed and slapped his two nephews on the back. "Isn't she a beauty? Her name is Victoria Rose."

Nadia heard Owen suck in a breath and lose a good portion of the color in his face. Her heart sank. Her family had done it to her again. Trouble had indeed followed the Kandrataviches home, and this time it came with four hooves. She raised an eyebrow at the mare, who was certainly a beauty. "What's Victoria Rose doing in IRS's corral?"

"It's her home now." Rupa held out a lump of sugar for Victoria Rose.

"How did she get here?" Nadia frowned as the horse took the cube. She could visualize the long line of champions who had produced this little lady.

"Wyatt Marshall just delivered her for us."

"I don't mean how she got here." She glanced heavenward and prayed for patience or a miracle. "I want to know *why* she is here."

"Oh, that's easy," said Stevo, her twenty-three-year-old brother. "I won her."

"Won her?" cried Nadia. "How did you win her?"

"Aces over tens beats queens over fours any day."

Owen choked and Nadia cried, "Poker! You won her in a poker game?" She knew she should have kept a closer eye on her brothers. They were constantly in trouble.

"Fair and square, Nadia. I didn't do anything wrong. Wyatt was the one dealing, not me."

"Well, take her back."

"I will not—she's mine." Stevo patted the back pocket of his jeans and smiled. "And I've got the papers to prove it."

Nadia glanced wildly around and pounced on the first question that popped into her mind. "Where did you get the money to play poker?" At Stevo's guilty look she glanced at Rupa's empty, battered old pickup truck, and her heart sank farther. "Where's the feed I sent you into town for first thing this morning?"

"I needed a start."

"You used the money I gave you to buy feed for IRS to bankroll your card game?"

"Someone had to back me, Nadia. And seeing as you're all for family, I figured you'd be right pleased to help me out."

"You figured wrong." She turned her attention to Rupa and her brother Gibbie. "What were you two doing while he was using my money to play some stupid card game?"

Both men shuffled their feet and stared at the ground. "Don't be mad at them, Sis," said Stevo. "It was all my idea."

Rupa noisily cleared his throat. "We helped him, Nadia."

The color Owen's lovemaking had put into her

cheeks faded. "How did you help him? It only takes one man to play a hand of cards."

"We just stood in the corner of the hardware store," explained Gibbie.

"Doing what?"

"They stood in front of the soda machine for forty-five minutes trying to figure it out." Stevo glanced at his younger brother and uncle and smiled. "They pretended that they had never seen one before."

Nadia glared at Owen as he burst out laughing. There wasn't a damn thing funny about any of this. She glanced helplessly at Victoria Rose. What was she supposed to do now? "So what you are telling me is that we now have two horses to feed with no food for either one of them?"

"Not exactly." Stevo looked at his brother Gibbie and grinned. "We stopped at the feed store, just like you told us to."

"So where's the feed?"

"They'll be delivering it later this afternoon."

"The feed mill won't deliver a few bags of oats way out here."

"I ordered more than a few. Victoria Rose is my horse, and I will take excellent care of her."

"Well, I hope you won the feed during your poker game, because I don't have the kind of money it will take to pay for the delivery of more than a couple of bags."

"I won something better than horse feed, Sis."

"What?"

"Money." He dug into his pocket and pulled out a wad of bills. "English green bucks, Sis." He waved the stack of bills. "Lots of English green bucks." He handed Nadia the money. "I already paid for the feed, and the rest is going to buy fencing for the south pasture." He stuck out his chest. "You told me this is my ranch, too, Nadia. I want to do my part and help."

Nadia's fingers shook as she clutched at the stack of bills in her hand. "I know you want to help, Stevo. But you have to do it honestly. You can't go around paying for everything with poker winnings."

"It was won honestly. Big-shot Wyatt Marshall thought he had suckered some green little immigrant kid with more money than brains into being the fifth man in their weekly game in the back room of the hardware store. Hell, he even let me win the first couple of hands. It wasn't my problem that I wasn't so green."

Nadia looked at Owen for help. He seemed a little dazed and in awe of Stevo, but maybe he could explain the hazards of poker playing. "Owen, what do you think?"

Owen studied Nadia's younger brother. He did in fact look fresh off the boat. Wyatt had a reputation for playing some fast ones on innocent people. Maybe it was time for the tables to be turned. He glanced at Victoria Rose and frowned; she had been Wyatt's pride and joy. Stevo was either the luckiest man with a deck of cards or the slickest. It didn't matter which—

Wyatt had pegged Stevo for an easy mark. "Wyatt Marshall does have a weekly card game going in the back of the hardware store."

"I don't doubt that he does. I want to know if this is legal." She waved the bills at Owen. She didn't need the law throwing Stevo in the slammer. With her luck the rest of the family would try to break him out.

"Sure, I don't see why not. They would have taken your brother's money without batting an eye."

"It was my money, not Stevo's," snapped Nadia. "What about the horse?"

"If Stevo has the legal papers all signed and sitting in his back pocket like he claims, then I don't see a problem." He glanced at the exquisite mare and shook his head. "Victoria Rose is now the reigning queen of the Kandratavich Ranch."

Stevo, Gibbie, and Rupa slapped Owen on the back as they made their way into the barn to check out the empty stall next to IRS.

Nadia glanced between Owen and the money clutched in her hand. It wasn't as much as she had first feared when Stevo had handed her the wad. Stevo had placed two fifties on either end of the wad and jammed all the singles and fives in between. Even so, there did seem to be a lot of twenties and tens jammed in there too. It was a lot of money. "So what do I do now?"

Owen gazed at her mouth. It was still red and swollen from his kisses. "Check out the south pasture and see what it needs, I guess." He walked over to the fence and watched Victoria Rose trot around the small corral. Wyatt Marshall had to be furious if not downright murderous at this very moment. The little mare was his favorite and almost guaranteed to be worth her weight in gold. She was old enough to breed next spring, and speculation had begun on who the first lucky stallion would be. It looked liked IRS had won that privilege.

Nadia leaned against the peeling fence and studied Owen, not the mare. "What's wrong?"

"Wyatt Marshall isn't known for his pleasantness." He reached over and pulled a piece of straw from her hair. She looked as if she had been rolling around in the hay kissing someone. She would have been doing a hell of a lot more than that if Victoria Rose hadn't made her appearance. Next time he would make sure there was no way they would be disturbed.

"Should I expect trouble?"

"Legally there isn't much he can do." He lifted another piece of hay from her hair. He was beginning to love the stuff.

"Do you think he'd try anything illegal?"

"Short of stealing her back, there's nothing he can do. Since your brother has the papers on her, he wouldn't chance it. The law is on your side."

Nadia didn't like the look of concern in Owen's eyes. "What do you think he'll do?" She had never met Mr. Marshall, but she had met plenty of his kind before.

"My guess is he'll try to make trouble for you and your family in town."

"What kind of trouble?" Trouble seemed to be the family's middle name. It had followed them along the back roads of Europe, across the Atlantic, and now to Crow's Head, North Carolina.

"He probably spread some stories about your family." He reached for her hand. "You know the kind. Any type of trouble that occurs in Crow's Head will be your family's fault. He'll try to pick fights over nothing and maybe even try to get someone fired from their job."

Nadia laughed. "That's all?"

"Isn't that enough?"

"Owen, where have you been? We are Gypsies." She reached up and kissed his surprised mouth. "Everyone always comes to us first when there's trouble. If someone's house is broken into, they come to our camp to see if we're hiding the missing television. If someone's daughter runs away, they come to our camp to see if one of our men kidnapped her. Even if someone's dog takes sick and dies, they accuse us of placing the evil eye on the poor animal."

"That's discrimination!"

"That's life, Owen." She toyed with the fine dusting of dark hair covering his forearm. "Didn't you realize that ten minutes ago you were about to make love to an outcast?"

A rakish smile brightened his face as he crowded her against the peeling fence. "For an outcast you kiss like an angel."

"I wasn't trying to be an angel." Her lower lip pouted.

He captured the sulking lip with his mouth and gave it a gentle tug before releasing it. "What were you trying to be, Nadia?" He cupped her cheek and tenderly stroked the smooth skin. "I've seen you as a talented musician, a superb horsewoman, a dutiful daughter, a warm and loving aunt, and a strict but caring older sister." With the tips of his fingers he brushed a dark curl away from her intense eyes. "Who was the woman that I held in my arms?"

"She was a woman, Owen. Just a woman."

SEVEN

Nadia stared out of the French doors of Owen's office and sadly shook her head at the confusion reigning on his lawn. Every female member of her family over the age of seven was in her most colorful Gypsy clothes busily running from here to there. No one seemed to be accomplishing a whole lot. Three colorful tents had been set up near the tennis court, and a lengthy buffet table crowded the patio. Dozens of small tables with colorful umbrellas and chairs had been rented and scattered about. It looked more like a carnival than an annual garden-club luncheon. What ever had possessed her to talk her family into catering this affair? "I don't know, Owen. This might not have been such a bright idea."

"Relax." He came up behind her and wrapped an arm around her waist. "It was my idea, so if anything goes wrong, I'll take the blame."

"Are you sure anyone is going to show up?"

"Aunt Verna says that if only half the people show

up who said they were going to, there won't be any room to walk." He gently kissed her wrinkled brow. "She's in the kitchen right now, taste-testing everything in sight."

Nadia leaned back against his warmth. "It was awfully nice of your aunt to hire my family to cater this affair, but I'm afraid she might be asking for trouble with the fortune-telling."

"Nonsense. Verna's beside herself with glee. She's finally one up on the snooty Violet DuBois. Imagine having this entire affair catered by Gypsies and not having their music and fortune-telling."

"She already paid my mom and my aunts a small fortune for the food. There really wasn't any need to hire two of my cousins to help park cars, my brother-in-law to play the violin, or Yelena to dance. And what about the fortune-telling?"

"What about it?" He hugged her closer. "How do you expect Verna to outdo the haughty Ms. Violet with just plain food and no entertainment?"

"What did Violet do last year? Hire the Philharmonic Orchestra?"

"Something much worse." He nuzzled her neck with his mouth. "She hired the Highland Marching Band, who practically deafened the entire club with their bagpipes blaring all afternoon. Poor Verna came home with a headache that lasted two days."

Nadia chuckled. "Well, I can guarantee that Gustavo's violin playing won't cause any headaches, but I have to warn you, Owen, some people don't take too kindly to having their fortune told."

"Relax." He quickly kissed the pout forming on her lower lip. "Your mom and Verna have it all figured out. The fortune-tellers are not part of the package. If anyone wants to have his fortune told, they are available to him, but he must pay the teller's fee. That way no one can blame Verna for a bad prediction."

"What if it's a good prediction?" Ever since their near-lovemaking in the barn two weeks ago, Owen had practically lived at the ranch. He was friendly toward her family and always there to lend a hand. He had helped Stevo and Rupa dig postholes for the south pasture, and he even got her father and Uncle Yurik jobs with his construction company. The Kandrataviches' luck was starting to change for the better, and all because of Owen. Her music hadn't returned yet, but it would. She had faith.

"Any good prediction I'm sure Verna will take full credit for." He opened the doors and gently pushed Nadia out onto the patio. "After all, this is her party." He glanced at the three tents set up by the tennis courts. "I've never had my fortune read." He contemplated the tents for another minute. "Which do you recommend—palm reading, tea leaves, or the tarot cards?"

Nadia nervously glanced around for something to do. "I'm sure you're going to be too busy for any of that nonsense." She didn't need any of her well-meaning relations playing matchmaker. People were very susceptible to what a dark-eyed Gypsy could read in the future. If she said to beware because there could be a car accident in the near future, the person would be so nervous every time he drove that he would probably *cause* the accident. If someone hinted that Owen would fall in love with a dark-eyed Gypsy, marry, and have many fine children, Owen could fall prey to the suggestion. She didn't need any more complications in her life right now. She had no idea where her relationship with Owen was going, but a trip down some rose-petal-strewn aisle was out of the question. It didn't matter that his kisses turned her knees to water or that every night it was becoming harder and harder not to invite him to stay. Her first concern had to be family. They were the ones who needed her. It didn't matter what she needed. Right now she had to concentrate on getting through this day without some major catastrophe. Then there was her music and album to worry about. Owen would just have to take a number and wait his turn.

"Why don't you want me to get my fortune told?"

"Oh, look, there's Yelena." Nadia nodded toward her sister, who was struggling with a card table and two folding chairs. "I have to go help her. I'll see you around, Owen." Not waiting for a response, she dashed off to help her sister.

Owen frowned as he stared after her. She looked enchantingly wild and sexy dressed in her native clothes. The colorful skirt swirled around her ankles; the white peasant blouse was pulled off her shoulders, giving him an enticing view of dusky smooth skin that seemed to beg for his kisses. He had never seen Nadia wear so much gold jewelry. Rings flashed on every one of her fingers, large hoop earrings dangled from her ears, and what appeared to be a fortune's worth of gold coins hung around her neck on fine gold chains. She even had a delicate bracelet wrapped around her ankle. When she had showed up with the rest of her family, it had taken every ounce of willpower not to haul her upstairs to his room and make sweet, passionate love to her all day. He noticed the way she worried her lower lip when he mentioned getting his fortune told. A sure sign she was upset about something. Why should she be upset? It was his fortune he wanted read, not hers.

"Excuse me, sir." Sebastian approached the slate patio with his usual bland composure. "Your presence is required in the kitchen for a moment."

Owen glanced away from Nadia and her sister. "Is there a problem, Sebastian?"

"Milly is threatening to quit, sir."

"Why would she do that?" Milly had been their cook for over thirty years and had never once voiced any concerns about leaving.

"It seems she's a trifle upset with Ms. Kandratavich's family and the way they cook."

"What's wrong with the way they cook?" He started for the house with Sebastian in tow.

"Two members of Ms. Kandratavich's family and

your aunt are in the side garden picking some more ingredients for their salad."

"Surely Milly's not upset because they are helping themselves to some of her vegetables?"

"Sir, they are not in the vegetable garden." He rolled his eyes and grimaced. "They are in the *flower* garden."

"Oh, Ida! You simply must have your palm read." Maybelle Lanston held out her liver-spotted hand. "See that line right there?" She pointed to her palm. "The darling little Gypsy told me there will be five great loves in my life."

Owen edged himself closer to the elderly pair and examined his own palm. Could a person really see how many loves you were going to have simply by looking at your palm? Maybe he should go pay a visit to Nadia's sister, Yelena, the resident palmist.

"Well, that just goes and proves how you wasted your five dollars," scolded Ida. "You've only been married four times, and as far as I know, you married *all* your great loves. Lord knows you married every man who even looked at you." Ida scooped a serving spoonful of what appeared to be some type of potato salad onto her plate. She sniffed it delicately, took a small taste, and proceeded to load on a couple more spoonfuls.

Maybelle gave a small huff. "I mentioned the fact that I had only had four husbands, and do you know what she said?" Ida glanced heavenward and went on to the next dish. "She said that as long as I was alive, there was always hope."

Owen started to choke. He hastily reached for a glass of water.

"You're eighty-one years old; who in their right mind would want you?" said Ida.

"You're just jealous."

"Of what?"

"You're jealous because you've only had two husbands, and Neville Walker was giving me the eye last Sunday in church." Maybelle brushed by Ida and headed for a table where two other ladies already sat.

Owen lost control of his laughter as Ida muttered, "You're as blind as an old bat, Maybelle. Neville Walker has been giving me the eye every Sunday since Reverend Howland gave that sermon about the sins of the flesh." She finished loading her plate and stomped after Maybelle.

Owen shook his head in amazement and glanced around the yard. Everyone who'd said they would come had, and by the looks of things they all must have brought a friend. Aunt Verna's party was a huge success. It was going to take a miracle for Violet to outdo this party next year. He had glimpsed Nadia only twice since the guests started to arrive, and both times she had been hurrying between the kitchen and the buffet table. He missed her. With a devilish gleam in his eye he started for the side entrance that led to the kitchen. Maybe it was time for him to check on the hired help.

He entered the kitchen and halted. Nadia was standing by the stove waving a wooden spoon and shouting something in a foreign language to one of her aunts. Her mother and another aunt waved their spoons and shouted back. He had no idea what all the fighting was about, but he was thankful that Milly's cutlery set was at the other end of the room. He stepped closer to Nadia. "Hi, need any help?"

Nadia lowered her spoon and glared at the other women.

"How about a referee?" joked Owen.

Nadia's mother started to say something in a foreign language to Owen.

"English, Olenka. I don't understand Russian." Owen offered a hesitant smile.

"I was speaking in Polish, forgive me." She glared back at her daughter and folded her arms across her ample chest. "Owen will be our judge."

Owen swallowed hard. "Judge of what?" He didn't like the sound of this.

Nadia nodded her head and handed Owen the wooden spoon. She lifted the lid from the enormous pot simmering on the stove. "Tell us if you think it needs more salt."

"Salt?" He glanced at the pot in confusion. "All this is about salt?"

"Just taste it," snapped Nadia.

Owen glanced at the pot and then back at Nadia.

"Does it need more salt?" He had no idea where she stood on the issue, but he knew enough not to criticize the cooking of the woman he loved. And love her he did. He had been fooling himself with the notion that he was falling in love with Nadia. He had already fallen, and hard.

"*Nyet, nyet*," shouted Olenka. "Nadia, don't you dare tell him what you think. We need him to judge with his taste, not with his *sertze*."

Nadia glared at her mother and then turned to Owen. "Just taste it, please."

Owen sampled the stew. He glanced at all three women and tasted it again. He didn't pick up on any signals from Nadia, so he lowered the spoon and beamed. "It's delicious."

"But does it need more salt?" asked Olenka.

He handed Nadia the spoon. "No, I think it's perfect the way it is." He held his breath and waited.

Nadia looked at her mother and said something that suspiciously sounded like "I told you so" and threw herself into Owen's arms. She rained sweet little kisses down his jaw.

He held her tight and grinned. This was the first time Nadia had shown any type of affection toward him in front of her family. He had been waiting for this sign for the past two weeks, ever since the day they nearly made love to each other in the barn. Nadia was finally starting to open up to him. Maybe now he could discover the secrets in her eyes. He chuckled softly and pressed a chaste kiss on her forehead. "What would you have done if I said it needed more salt?"

She continued to smile as she stepped out of his arms and started to fill an empty tureen her sister Sonia had just brought in. "Added more salt."

Owen glanced at Sonia and frowned. The woman didn't belong on her feet; in fact, if he had to guess, he would say she belonged in some delivery room with a doctor standing over yelling, "Push, push." Sonia was pregnant, *very pregnant*. Owen had no idea that a woman could be that pregnant and not burst. When Sonia reached for the full tureen, Owen stepped in and took the heavy dish. "I'll take that for you." He smiled at Nadia and whispered a promise before heading back outside. "I'll see you later."

Nadia stood in the doorway for a long time after he was gone and stared into space.

Sofia stared into the teacup for a long time before lifting her head to look at Owen. "Do you want me to say what you want to hear, or do you want the truth?"

"I already know what I want to hear, so tell me the truth."

"You're a builder." She lowered the cup back onto the table before them.

Owen tried to hide his disappointment. He had expected better from Sofia. Everybody knew he was an architect and owned a construction company. It had taken him half the afternoon to decide which method of fortune-telling he would prefer. He had shame-lessly eavesdropped on every guest he could, trying to figure out which method seemed the best. The reactions were varied, and over half the guests had tried more than one method. In the end he had chosen Sofia by process of elimination. Yelena, Nadia's nineteen-year-old sister, seemed too sweet and innocent to answer any questions he might propose. Volga Yonkovich, the very pregnant Sonia's mother-in-law, told fortunes with the tarot cards. He wanted nothing to do with any deck of cards that contained cards entitled "The Hanged Man" and "Death." So that left Sofia, with her very predictable predictions.

"You're a builder of dreams."

Owen continued to frown. Of course he could be called a builder of dreams. Every house or building he built was somebody's dream.

"You not believe me?" questioned Sofia.

Disillusioned, he said, "Yes, I believe you, Sofia." Half a day's worry was for nothing. Nadia wasn't trying to protect him from the unknown future when she refused to talk about her family's fortune-telling. She had been trying to hide the fact that her family couldn't tell the future. He hadn't really expected Sofia to look at the leaves and tell him all his dreams would come true, but a little more hedging on her part would have been nice.

Sofia leaned back and studied the young man who had become so important to her niece. "I'm not talking about houses or office buildings."

"You're not?" Owen glanced at the old bone-china cup sitting in front of him. "What are you talking about, then?"

"You." She pushed aside the deep-purple velvet material that was covering the table and reached beneath it. She pulled out a tall glass of iced tea and took a sip. "You didn't come here to find out about your business, did you?"

"I already know about my business."

"It is very prosperous," said Sofia. She smiled knowingly and nodded her head. "It will continue to grow over the years because you will have many fine children who will help you."

Owen stared at the cup in astonishment. "You can tell all that by a few soggy tea leaves?"

"No. I use my gift of wisdom to know your business will prosper, and my gift of sight to know how much you love children. You are very kind to all the little ones at the ranch."

He flushed slightly at being that obvious. "So what do the tea leaves tell you?"

"They tell me you are building another dream. One that concerns your happiness."

"Will this dream come true?"

"I cannot see." She looked at Owen and added, "I can tell you that it is a very strong dream. One that is built from the heart."

Owen slowly stood up. "Thank you, Sofia."

"I disappointed you, didn't I?" She folded her hands and placed them in her lap. "You perhaps expected predictions of travel, great adventures, or chance encounters?" She sadly shook her head. "Forgive me, I had forgotten you are a *gadjo* and mistakenly gave you the truth instead of inventions."

He sighed and ran his fingers through his hair. How was he ever going to explain to Sofia what he had been searching for? "It is I who should ask for your forgiveness. I came here seeking an answer"—he gave a self-indulgent little laugh—"or at least a hint that I was on the right track."

Sofia smiled. "Your heart will tell you if you are on the right track. As for your dream"—her many bracelets jiggled as she spread her hands outward—"I cannot say what end will come." She softened her words with a smile. "Only you have the power to master your dreams."

Owen bowed slightly. "Thank you, Sofia." He turned toward the tent's opening. It was time to give someone else a chance to have their fortune told.

"Owen?" called Sofia softly.

"Yes?"

"Good luck with your dream." She smiled knowingly as he ducked out of the tent.

"What do you mean Sonia's having her baby?" shouted Owen. He glanced around the camp in astonishment. No one seemed to be in any great hurry to go anywhere. Where were the suitcase, the frantic husband, and the concerned grandparents? He looked at Nadia, who was helping to unload the leftover food from the garden-club luncheon. Everything at his house had been cleaned up and returned to order hours ago. He had made sure the rental company had come and picked up all the tables, chairs, and tents before driving out to Nadia's. "Where is she?"

"In bed where she belongs," said Nadia. She picked up the paper bag filled with garlic-flavored breads and started to walk toward one of the mobile homes.

"She belongs in a hospital!" shouted Owen. "Give me five minutes to run back to your house to get my car, and we'll take her."

Nadia frowned at Owen and lovingly placed a hand on one of her little cousin's shoulders. "Lower your voice, Owen. You're scaring the children."

Owen glanced at the little dark-eyed girl and frowned. She did look scared to death, but by his shouting? He had seen members of Nadia's family argue with one another, and to say they shouted would be an understatement. "Why am I scaring her?"

"Don't mention the word *hospital* again," whispered Nadia. She smiled encouragingly at the girl and handed her the paper bag to carry in. She waited until the child was out of earshot. "I know, in America everyone goes to the hospital for the simplest of reasons. But where we come from, we don't go to hospitals just because we have a cut or a sprain."

Owen glanced at the other mobile home, the one he knew Sonia was in. He started to get a sinking feeling in the pit of his stomach. "You don't go to hospitals to have babies, either, do you?"

"No. To most of my family, a hospital is the last resort. It usually means there is no other hope."

"Who's going to deliver the baby?"

"The same women who delivered her first two, my mother and Sasha."

"Your mother delivered her own grandchildren?"

"Can you think of a more caring person?"

"Caring is all well and good, but what about experience, training, and a big fat medical degree hanging on the wall?" His horror-stricken gaze remained on the mobile home. In the gathering dusk someone had turned on the inside lights in the back bedroom. Behind those walls Sonia was giving birth.

"What does a piece of paper hanging on the wall have to do with delivering a baby? Between my mother and Sasha, they must have delivered over two hundred babies."

"They're midwives?"

"To our people, yes, they are midwives." She glanced at him and smiled. "Relax, Owen. It shouldn't be that much longer."

Owen paled further. "She's been working all day carrying heavy serving dishes back and forth. All that work didn't make her go into labor, did it?"

"No, she was showing signs of labor earlier, Owen. We all knew, so we kept a close eye on her. We didn't let her carry the really heavy stuff."

"Why in the hell did you let her work, for cripe's sake?" He couldn't help it. Nothing in his life's experience sounded so cruel and heartless as watching a woman in labor wait on his aunt's rich and haughty friends.

"Because she wanted to," snapped Nadia. "The idea of watching my sister man the buffet table while labor was starting didn't appeal to me, either, Owen." She closed her eyes and sighed. Taking a deep breath, she sat down on the tailgate of her uncle's battered pickup truck. "She wanted to earn her share of the profits. Last month she saw a used crib for sale in one of the thrift shops in town. She has the cradle that her other two have outgrown, but she has her heart set on a crib for this one." She swung her feet and stared at the trailer, where new life was struggling to make its way into the world. "I offered to buy the crib for her, but she refused. She thinks I do too much for them as it is. Sonia has her share of the Kandratavich stubbornness."

Owen sat down next to her and contemplated the trailer. "What do we do now?"

"We wait." She smiled at Owen and took his hand. "Don't worry, bringing a baby into this world is a very natural thing for a woman."

"But what if . . ." His voice trailed off as a distant wail of a baby came from the trailer. He felt Nadia's hand tighten her grip, and everyone seemed to stop whatever they were doing and stare at the trailer.

A moment later a proud-looking father, Gustavo, came to the door carrying a small bundle wrapped in a soft blanket. "It's a girl!" He waited for the cheering to die down. "Mother and daughter are both fine and beautiful." He held the baby up and announced, "In honor of our daughter being the first Kandratavich born in America, we name her Liberty." He disappeared back into the trailer as more merriment erupted.

Owen turned to Nadia and wiped at the two tears rolling down her cheeks. He was afraid he was showing the same relief and happiness. His voice shook slightly, and he had to clear the lump out of his throat before he could ask, "Well, Aunt Nadia, what do we do now?"

She glanced around the camp and grinned. Her father and uncles were already pulling out the wine, and Celka and Sofia were piling the tables with food. Someone had picked up a violin and started to play a lively tune. "Now, Owen, we must share a great Gypsy tradition." She grabbed his hand and yanked him off the tailgate and toward the tables.

"What's that?"

"We celebrate!"

EIGHT

Owen stood in the darkness and burned. Each seductive sway of Nadia's hips pulled at his groin. The enticing flash of a bare calf or the provocative arch of her arms as she beckoned an imaginary lover sent another wave of heat pounding through his veins. Her dark hair flew behind her like a proud banner as she whirled and danced her way around the campfire. The faster the music played, the faster Nadia's bare feet flew over the grass.

Twice she brushed by him, bewitching him further with her dreamy smile and the flash of desire burning in her eyes. He prayed that her body was going to live up to the promises blazing in her eyes all night. Sometime today their relationship had changed. She was more open with him, allowing him nearer. The sweet little kisses from the kitchen had only been the beginning. All night long she had been next to him, holding his hand, touching his shoulder, or just smiling.

At first he thought she was caught up in the excitement of the celebration, but then he had begun to notice the differences between Nadia and her family. The wine was flowing freely between the adults, but he had only seen her take one glass, the same amount as he. The storytelling had gone from questionable to farfetched. She had enjoyed the stories, but she hadn't contributed any of her own. The stories reminded him of a bunch of fishermen trying to outdo one another with accounts of the size of the fish that had gotten away. Even though she laughed in all the right places, it didn't take a psychic to know her mind wasn't on the tales. And by the smoldering glances she had been casting his way all evening, he had a feeling he knew what she was thinking. The same thing he'd been thinking all night: hot endless kisses that lasted all night and into the morning. He did not want to go home to spend another sleepless night in a bed that suddenly seemed too big for just one man.

Nadia whirled faster as the music built toward a climax. Her eyes were closed, and her arms reached upward into the darkness. The glow of the fire gleamed off the brilliant colors woven into her skirt, and her hair radiated the dancing flames. Her rounded breasts heaved against the low-cut blouse straining to be free, and the gentle clinking of her jewelry beckoned his senses. Nothing in his life had prepared him for the vision of watching Nadia dance. She was primitive and wild. She had become one with the music. The passion, the need, the desire, vibrated around her, calling to her imaginary lover. Calling to him.

In a final frenzy the music and Nadia came to a sudden stop. Gustavo slowly lowered his violin as Nadia bowed her head and breathed deeply. Owen held his breath and waited as her family applauded.

Nadia slowly raised her head and glanced across the fire to encounter Owen's hungry gaze. Her eyes darkened to black pools of need, and her harsh breathing turned more ragged. She ignored her family and the shouts for more wine. On soundless feet she crossed the packed dirt and grass and stood before Owen. "I danced for you."

He felt himself drowning in the honesty swimming in her eyes. "I never had a woman dance for me before." He reached out and tenderly drew a line down her flushed cheek. Her skin was hot and damp under his finger. She felt like a woman who had just spent the last hour making love. "Thank you. I will treasure the memory always."

"Do you understand what it means when a woman dances for a special man?"

Owen glanced away from the desire burning in her eyes and toward the campfire. Nadia's family were busy passing another wine bottle, and Yurik was in the middle of another story. They seemed to have forgotten Nadia and Owen as the celebration continued. He stepped back farther into the night, taking Nadia with him. "Does it mean that you are attracted to me?"

She moved in closer to him. The cool evening breeze whipped her skirt around one of his pants legs, binding them together. "It means I want you." She pressed her palms against his chest and stared up into his handsome face. The shadows were too thick to see his reaction. "I need you, Owen." Her voice shook with that need. "I need you more than my next breath." Her hands trembled, and her knees wobbled as she declared the extent of her feelings. "I need you more than my music."

Owen closed the door behind him and slowly lowered Nadia's feet to the kitchen floor. He had carried her the entire quarter-mile from the camp because she was barefooted, and he didn't want to waste any precious moments looking for her sandals. With the turn of the lock they left the Kandratavich Ranch and her family on the other side. There were only he and Nadia; nothing beyond the door mattered. Tonight there weren't going to be any interruptions.

Nadia leaned her cheek against his chest and listened to his pounding heart. "I told you I was too heavy to carry all the way back here."

"We made it, didn't we?" His fingers teased the elastic neckline of her blouse.

"I had my doubts coming up that last hill." She pressed her lips to the thundering pulse still hammering in his throat.

A faint tremor shook his body. "That was your fault, not mine." He brushed back a lock of her hair and tenderly stroked the curve of her cheek. "You should never play with a man's ear as he's carrying you up a *mountain*."

Laughter sparkled in her eyes as she gazed at the ear she'd been nibbling on. "I couldn't help myself." She ran a finger over the lobe and smiled. "Being carried up that *itsy-bitsy* hill was the most romantic thing that ever happened to me." She reached up and gave a playful nip to the ear.

"It wouldn't have been so romantic if I'd dropped you." He shuddered as her teeth grazed his lobe.

Nadia chuckled and blew against the moist skin. "I'm sure we could have thought of something while we were lying on the ground."

Owen once again swept her up in his arms and turned off the kitchen light. The faint glow of the night-light plugged in at the bottom of the stairs guided him across the room. "Will you think it's romantic if I carry you up these stairs?"

"I don't know, Owen." Her lips brushed his throat where his pulse pounded. She loved teasing him. "We could both break our necks if you don't make it."

"If you don't stop that"—he shifted her weight so that her mouth was farther away from his throat—"we'll never make it up these steps." He started to climb the stairs.

Nadia chuckled softly and laid her head against his shoulder. "I hear huffing and puffing."

"You think this is huffing and puffing?" He looked down into her smiling face and wiggled his eyebrows. "Give me a couple of minutes, and I'll show you huffing and puffing." He stepped onto the landing and stopped.

Nadia nodded her head in the direction of one of the doors. She tucked in her feet as Owen carried her over the threshold. Her fingers fumbled for a moment before locating the light switch. Light flooded the room as Owen lowered her feet once again to the floor. Her feet touched the cool white tile, and she glanced around the room and tried viewing it through Owen's eyes. What will he think of her outlandish sense of decorating? Maybe she shouldn't have tried to be so American.

Owen blinked against the sudden flaring of light, and then he blinked again at the room. Nadia hadn't taken him to her bedroom. They were standing in the middle of her bathroom. A bathroom that was decorated with one main motif, Mickey Mouse. Nadia had livened up the plain, sterile white room with America's favorite mouse. The shower curtain was clear except for the foot-high Mickeys splashed all over it. Bright red-and-black towels draped the towel bars, two red throw rugs dotted the floor, red-and-white polka-dotted curtains hung at the window, and a metal trash can with MICKEY printed on it sat near the sink. She had hung two framed posters on the walls. One with Mickey and Minnie kissing with hearts decorating the background and the other was a solo shot of Mickey as the Sorcerer's Apprentice from *Fantasia*.

The room told him something very important

about the person who had decorated it: Nadia had a delightful sense of humor buried underneath all her worries. She worried constantly about her family, about her music, and about money. But it took someone truly whimsical to do a bathroom à la Disney.

He glanced around the room one last time before smiling at the woman standing in front of him. "My compliments to the decorator."

She graciously nodded her head. "I'm sure Walt would have appreciated that."

He chuckled and tenderly cupped her cheek. "I was referring to you."

She softly closed the door, took off her belt, and dropped it on the tile floor. She started to unhook her jewelry and place it piece by piece in a ceramic dish sitting by the sink. "This stuff looks great with the outfit"—she slid the thick hoops from her ears—"but it weighs a ton."

He leaned back against the door and watched as she slowly seduced him again with the removal of each piece of jewelry. By the time she raised her foot and gently unclasped the ankle bracelet, he was going out of his mind. His hands itched to help her, but his fingers were trembling so badly, he knew he could never undo those tiny clasps.

Nadia stepped away from the sink weighing five pounds less. She held Owen's gaze as she pulled her blouse over her head and tossed it in the direction of the red hamper. "I've been working all day in the kitchen." Her fingers undid the button at the back of her skirt, and the colorful material pooled at her feet. She kicked it aside. "I smell like goulash and *kapusti*."

Owen forgot to breathe. She was standing in front of him wearing nothing more than a strapless white lace bra that barely covered her dark nipples and a scrap of blood-red silk shielding her womanhood.

She reached behind her back and unclasped the bra. Twin pale globes shifted their weight and bounced lightly. Dark, dusky nipples thrust themselves proudly from their creamy mounds. With a graceful move she slid the silk panties down her legs and lightly stepped out of them. She hooked them on one finger and sent them sailing to the pile of clothes already on the floor. She continued to gaze questionably at Owen. He seemed to be either in a daze or totally bewildered. Maybe she was being too assertive. Had she misjudged American women so wrongly? From her experience these past four years, American women weren't only assertive, they were direct, bold, and sometimes downright brazen. Maybe Owen preferred his women a little less brazen. Maybe she should have waited for him to undress her, but she was tired of waiting. She had waited for two weeks for him to make the next move, and he hadn't. Southern gentlemen be damned, she didn't want to wait any longer. She had been totally truthful with Owen earlier; she needed him more than she needed her music.

She gave Owen a hesitant, shy smile before stepping into the tub. "I could use somebody to scrub my back." She pulled the curtain and started the water.

Owen came out of his daze with a crash. She had just issued the best offer of his life, and all he could do was stand there with his mouth hanging open. She was more than beautiful; she had been breathtaking. He stared at her enticing form behind the shower curtain. The heavy plastic distorted her lush body, and the cheerful, grinning Mickeys seem to be printed in the most maddening of places. He kicked off his shoes and tore at the buttons on his shirt. Behind that ridiculous curtain was a sensational back crying out for his attention. His remaining clothes hadn't even hit the floor before he pushed aside the curtain and stepped into the tub with her.

Nadia pushed her streaming hair out of her eyes and glanced over her shoulder at Owen. Her imagination hadn't done him justice. He was superbly built, from his broad shoulders down to his muscular thighs and thick calves. The water splashing from the shower moistened the dark hair scattered over his body. The tiny beads of moisture winked and sparkled with each breath he took. Her gaze drifted down his chest, over his flat stomach, and fastened on his arousal thrusting out of the dark nest of curls. Owen stood in her tub hard and proud. Excitement danced through her body. She quickly glanced upward and mustered a small smile. She handed Owen a bar of soap, brushed her wet hair aside, and turned her back to him.

Owen lathered his hands, put down the soap, and

proceeded to wash Nadia's delicate back. The palms of his hands glided over the curve of her back, outlining her spine, the smoothness of her shoulders, and the flare of her hips. With each caress of his hands desire wound itself tighter until thinking became an impossibility. He could only feel, only respond.

Nadia trembled as Owen's slick hands teased the sides of her breasts. When they made a second pass up her sides, she leaned back farther into Owen and sighed as he cupped her breasts and tested their weight. Her nipples hardened more, bursting through the soapy lather and pressing into the palm of his hand. He gave them a tender squeeze before roaming lower and soaping her stomach, her hips, and the patch of curls between her thighs. She melted into his arms as his fingers teased and tormented the desire building there. Skilled fingers frolicked through the dense curls softly stroking the moist skin awaiting his touch and then retreating back into the bush.

She leaned her head against his shoulder and whispered, "*Pajalossta.*"

He chuckled and slid his hands back up to her straining breasts. "As much as I love hearing you talk in all those languages, I don't understand a single word you say." He lightly squeezed the globes overflowing his hands and captured the hard little berries of her nipples between his fingers. "Tell me what you want in English."

Nadia bit her lip against the pleasure spiraling through her body. "You, Owen, I want you."

Owen's mouth slid along the slippery curve of her shoulder as his arousal gently nudged her rounded bottom. "Are you ready to come out yet?" He was rock-hard, but he wasn't going to make love to her for the first time in some slippery tub. He wanted everything to be perfect. He wanted it slow and sweet and so satisfying that she would always remember their first time together.

Her breasts thrust farther into his hands, and her bottom twitched against him. "I haven't washed my hair yet."

"Your hair is perfect." He lifted a soaked strand and kissed it. The water darkened the dark brown tresses to jet black, and they wrapped their way around his wrist and clung there.

"My hair is already soaking wet. It will only take a minute to shampoo it." She glanced over her shoulder at Owen and pouted prettily. "I refuse to make love to you with hair that smells of cabbage."

He untangled his wrist, reached for the bottle of shampoo sitting on the side of the tub, and squirted a generous amount into his palm. "Is that what I've been smelling?" He pulled Nadia away from the direct spray of the shower and started to work the shampoo into her thick hair. "I hate to inform you of this, but the smell of cabbage can be very erotic."

Nadia closed her eyes and relished the seductive feel of Owen's fingers massaging her scalp. "If you think *kapusti* is erotic, I can't wait to see what you think of borscht."

He worked the rich lather through her hair. The enticing scent of apples filled the confined area. "On you it would have to smell delicious." He stepped under the spray, bringing her with him. The white bubbles cascaded from her hair, drifted down her back, over her rounded bottom, down her incredible legs, and down the drain. He ran his fingers through her silken hair and released the last of the bubbles to follow the same path. Lucky bubbles. "There"—he moved Nadia away from the spray—"you don't smell like cabbage any longer."

"Good." Nadia reached for the bar of soap and gently started to lather his chest. "It's my turn to torture you." Her hands slid lower. She chuckled softly as her fingers worked the lather through the coarse hair surrounding his shaft.

"I don't think this is such a good idea, Nadia." He reached for her hands.

Her fingers avoided being captured as one hand slid lower and cupped him while the other fingers tenderly wrapped around the thrusting shaft. She smiled triumphantly as he threw back his head and thrust deeper into her hands. Her lips skimmed his chest with light kisses. "You were saying?"

Owen tried to breathe as violent shudders shook his body. Her delicate little finger had begun to move, and it was tearing him apart. "I said you are a witch."

Nadia released his hard little nipple from between her teeth and glanced up. A wondrous smile lit up her face. "I do believe I'm beginning to like that word."

Her smile had done him in. He couldn't handle one more moment of her sweet torture. In a flurry of motion he swept her up into his arms, turned off the shower, and stepped out of the tub. He stood her up on one of the red throw rugs and tossed her a towel. "You have exactly one minute to dry off."

She grinned and used the towel to wrap her hair in turban style. "I can't dry my hair in one minute." She reached for the last towel and started to dry her arms and face.

Owen finished briskly rubbing his aching body and tossed his damp towel back onto the rack. "You have ten seconds left."

The big thick red towel caressed her stomach and legs. She was patting her toes dry when Owen swept her back up into his arms and opened the bathroom door. "Time's up!"

Nadia clutched at Owen's warm, dry body. "Why the hurry?" Seeing his confused look as he stepped out into the darkened hall, she pointed over her shoulder to her bedroom door.

"Because I could stand only sixty seconds of watching you dry yourself off. Another second and we would have been on the floor finishing what you started in the tub." He walked into the room still carrying her. He made out the shape of her bed in the darkened room and quickly crossed the floor, then slowly started to lower her to the bed.

"Me!" She felt the comforting softness of the quilt

meet her naked back and the warmth of Owen's body as it slowly covered her.

"Yes, you"—his mouth fastened on one of her nipples, and he gently tugged—"you little witch."

Nadia stroked his back and cupped the tight muscles in his buttocks. Her thighs gently parted for his seeking fingers. "Now I know I love that word." She arched her back and raised her hips as his fingers found her moist passion. The curls guarding her passion might still be damp from the shower, but the moisture his fingers were gathering had nothing to do with water and everything to do with Owen. Her thighs moved farther apart as his fingers slid deep inside, testing her, tormenting her. "Owen, *pajaloosta!*" Her head moved from side to side on the pillow, loosening the towel and sending her damp hair in every direction. Her hips jerked upward as he removed his fingers, leaving her empty and aching. "Please, Owen."

He moved up her body and allowed his forearms to take most of his weight. His manhood nudged at the moist opening. "Are you ready for me, Nadia? I don't want to hurt you."

She clutched at his hips and tugged him forward. "I'm hurting now, Owen." She wrapped her legs around his thighs and urged him on. "Stop the ache inside me."

"It will be my pleasure." He softly kissed her mouth and eased himself slowly inside her. Her silky softness closed around him like a hundred greedy fingers. His back arched with satisfaction when he was completely inside her heat. "Oh, Nadia." He groaned. "What sweet pleasure it is." He felt the hot, slick walls tighten around him and plunged deeper. Again and again. He couldn't get enough of her. Her sweet heat and the tiny little moans she was making were driving him out of his mind. He wanted it all. He needed it all.

Her thighs tightened, and her fingers dug into his back as the rhythm increased and the heat escalated out of control. She met each thrust and greedily demanded more. The pressure built until there was no more room left inside her. It erupted into a body-shattering explosion. The climax started at her core, where their bodies were joined, and radiated outward. It shook her fingertips, and the thighs clasping Owen shuddered.

He felt the small contractions gripping him tighter, thrust one last time, and joined Nadia in release.

She lay there in the dark with his body covering hers and listened to his breathing. Her fingers gently stroked his damp, quaking body. He had felt the explosion too. Everything she had heard, read, or learned about sex over the years had been destroyed. Nothing had prepared her for Owen. His name tumbled from her lips in wonder: "Owen."

He leaned up on his elbows and brushed her damp hair away from her face. "Hmmm . . ." The only light in the room came from the pale moonshine barely making its way in through the windows. He couldn't see her expression clearly, but he had to be squashing her with his weight. He started to move off her.

Nadia tightened her hold. "Don't." She liked the feel of his body covering hers, but she loved the feel of him being inside her. They were still joined.

"I'm too heavy for you."

"No, you're not." She refused to loosen her grip. "You feel perfect to me."

He gave a halfhearted chuckle and tried to regain control over his breathing. "There is no way I'm going to smother you, so hold on." In a graceful movement he rolled over, carrying Nadia with him.

She unwrapped her thighs, pulled up her knees, and ended up straddling his hips as he settled back down onto the bed. She could still feel the bulk of his manhood resting inside her. Her head found his shoulder, and one of her hands lay on his chest. She could feel each beat of his heart with her fingertips. "You make a wonderful pillow." She snuggled up closer, yawned, and closed her eyes. "It's been a long day." Her voice faded away as another yawn overtook her.

Owen's arms cradled her warm body next to his heart. He silently cursed as his body responded to the moist sweetness still surrounding him. Nadia was practically asleep on top of him. She deserved it. He knew for a fact that she'd been up since before dawn helping her family get ready for the luncheon, then she worked all afternoon waiting on the social elite, and then had spent hours cleaning it all up. To top that off, she'd been given another niece, and the traditional Kandratavich celebration that had followed would have made a stronger person buckle under the weight of flowing wine, platters of food, music, and dance. He and Nadia had left the celebration sometime after one in the morning and the party was still going strong. He had to give the Kandrataviches credit, they sure knew how to celebrate a new arrival with style. He visualized Nadia dancing around the blazing campfire, seducing him with her eyes and body.

His arms tightened around the woman curled upon his chest as all his blood rushed to his loins.

Nadia wiggled slightly as he grew inside her, stretching the walls of her womanhood with a sweet ache. She slowly rocked her hips and smiled dreamily as he clutched at her thighs and turned to solid hardness deep inside her. Her breath feathered his neck as she reached up and nibbled on his ear.

Owen groaned. "Nadia." He told his body to behave, but his hips bucked upward. "Are you asleep?"

"Shhh . . ." Hundreds of kisses covered his face and throat. "If I am, this is the most wonderful dream I ever had, and I don't want to be awakened." She rocked her hips faster and arched her back.

His gaze fastened on her pale breasts jutting outward. His fingers guided her hips into a wilder pace as his mouth reached for the protruding, rigid nipples.

Nadia felt his mouth tug at her breasts and went over the edge. The spiraling climax left her reeling and clutching the only solid thing she could reach: Owen.

Her name was a hoarse shout—"Nadia!"—as he thrust upward and spilled his release deep inside her.

He tenderly cradled her damp body onto his chest as she collapsed. He had to wait until his breathing returned to a semblance of normal before he could jokingly ask, "Are you asleep now?"

"Shhh . . ." He could feel her smile against his collarbone. "I just had the most spectacular dream."

He chuckled and brushed a handful of her now-dried hair away from his face. The exquisite tresses slid through his fingers like fine silk. "You, my little Gypsy, are definitely a witch." His lips kissed her smooth forehead. "A gorgeous, seductive, and lovable witch." It was the closest he would come to saying he loved her. He knew that any words of commitment would have her bolting like some frightened rabbit.

Nadia nestled closer and smiled. "I do believe I love that word." She closed her eyes and gave a delicate little yawn.

Owen's arms tightened fractionally for a few minutes before they naturally slackened as sleep overtook him. They both fell asleep, in the heat of the night, still joined.

Nadia slowly opened her eyes and squinted at the daylight streaming in through the windows. She noticed two things immediately. One was the light sheet covering her, and the other was the soft pillow under her head instead of Owen's solid chest. She preferred Owen's chest. She wiggled her nose and took a deep whiff of air. Somewhere close by was coffee! She turned her head and sat up. Owen was standing in front of her bureau studying the aged black-and-white photographs she had stuck into the frame around the mirror. The only thing he was wearing were the faded, tight jeans he had on last night. He had pushed aside some of her stuff and made room for the tray loaded down with two cups of coffee, a jar of strawberry preserves, and a basket full of Aunt Sofia's famous muffins. She frowned at the muffins for a moment before asking, "Is the coffee still hot?"

Owen quickly turned around and grinned. She was as breathtakingly beautiful as when he had left the bed a half hour earlier. Her hair had dried into a wild mass of curls tumbling past her shoulders, her mouth was still red and ripe from their lovemaking, and her eyes were as dark and mysterious as ever. His gaze slid downward and hotly admired the creamy fullness of her breasts. He chuckled as she hastily pulled the sheet up to her throat. "I just made it."

She glanced at the tray. "Did you make the muffins too?"

"Nope." He picked up the tray and carried it toward the bed. "I can't take credit for them." He placed the tray on her lap, walked over to the other side of the bed, dropped his pants to the floor, and carefully slid under the sheet.

Nadia steadied the tray as the bed shifted under his weight. "May I be so bold as to ask you where you found a basket full of Sofia's muffins?"

"You may ask me anything you want." He picked up a muffin, sliced it through the middle, and spread globs of homemade strawberry preserves over both pieces. He handed one to Nadia and grinned. "She gave it to me." He bit into the muffin and moaned with delight.

Nadia stared at her half. "When did you run into Sofia?"

"When I was downstairs making us coffee." He took another bite. "All I could find was instant. I hope it's okay."

"All I have is instant." She glanced at Owen as he polished off the rest of his muffin. "Are you saying Sofia was in the kitchen when you went down?"

"Nope." He cut into another muffin. "She knocked on the door while I was down there."

"And you opened it!" *Great, just great!* "Didn't it ever occur to you about how that must have looked?" She shook the muffin at him, sending crumbs scattering across the sheet. "You answering my door, half dressed, the first thing in the morning?"

He casually reached for his cup of coffee. "She already knew I was here."

"How did she know that?"

"My car has been parked outside your door all night." He took a sip of coffee and studied Nadia. He hadn't been real thrilled when Sofia came knocking, but the choices were either ignore the knock and make a fool out of himself, Nadia, and Sofia or confront the situation. He had decided to confront the situation.

Nadia finally bit into her muffin. "What did she say?"

"She said that you liked strawberry preserves on your muffins and that you take your coffee with cream, no sugar." He couldn't prevent the grin that was teasing his mouth. He watched, entranced, as Nadia finished the muffin and slowly licked the strawberry preserves that had coated her fingertips. His gaze turned feverish as he thought about what else they could do with strawberry preserves.

"She didn't say anything else?"

"She said lots of stuff." He moved in closer and prepared another muffin for her. His coarse thigh brushed against her smooth, naked one. He owed Sofia a big, heartfelt thank-you the next time he saw her. Breakfast in bed had been her idea. When she had knocked, he was in the kitchen quietly searching in vain for a coffeepot for himself. He was going to allow Nadia all the sleep she wanted. He hadn't liked the dark circles that had appeared under her eyes recently. But Sofia entered the kitchen like a whirlwind, gathering up a tray, finding the jar of instant coffee in the back of the refrigerator, and explaining how Nadia took her coffee. It appeared Sofia had been on the right track. What woman wouldn't love breakfast in bed?

"What kind of stuff?" She finished her coffee and the remaining muffin.

"I don't know." He swallowed hard as the sheet slid farther down. The gentle slope of her breasts came into full view, and her nipples appeared to be dark shadows under the light sheet. He took the tray and, leaning over Nadia, placed it on the floor. His finger dipped into the preserves before sitting back up. "Half of what she was saying was in some foreign language. I think Russian."

Nadia watched his jam-smeared finger as it softly stroked the curve of her breast to her nipple, leaving a trail of strawberry preserves behind. He ran the back of his finger down the other breast, giving it the same treatment. Her gaze followed his finger as it lifted to his mouth, and he licked the tip clean. "Owen, what are you doing?"

"Having breakfast in bed."

A smile played at the corner of her mouth. "We already had breakfast in bed."

"No, we didn't." He pulled the sheet lower so that it fell onto her lap, leaving her breasts bare to his gaze. "That was an appetizer." His tongue licked the gooey trail of jam from her breast before his mouth captured one strawberry-coated nipple and sucked it clean. His hungry gaze shot up to hers. "This is breakfast."

Nadia melted under his tender assault. Her arms reached for him as she whispered, "I'll take one of everything on the menu."

NINE

Owen glared down at Nadia's father, lying in the hospital bed, and raised his voice slightly. "You will stay in that bed until the doctor says you can get up." He gently pushed Milosh back down. "If I have to tie you to these rails, I will."

"I go home now," said Milosh.

"Not tonight." His eyes sympathetic, he sadly shook his head. "You heard what the doctor said."

"Doctor, shmoctor, what does he know? He's only a young kid."

Owen pulled the chair he had been sitting in earlier closer to the bed and sat down. "Listen, Milosh, I know this is hard for you, being in the hospital and all, but it's for your own good."

"Going home will do me better good."

Owen chuckled, "You're thick-headed, Milosh."

"So the kid doctor told me when he took those fancy pictures of my head." Milosh grinned and rubbed the side of his head where a huge lump had formed.

"He said that steel beam should have killed me, not just dented my head a little bit."

Owen frowned, quickly stood up, and marched over to the window. He didn't want Milosh to see the emotions tearing through him. The father of the woman he loved had almost been killed at his construction site. For two weeks he and Nadia had been lovers, spending every night together. He knew they were growing closer, but now there was this. When he had seen Milosh's crumpled, unconscious body lying on the ground, he had wanted to die. How was he ever going to explain to Nadia that her father died working for his company? The hardest thing he'd ever had to do was to call Nadia from the emergency room twenty minutes ago and explain about the accident. She and her mother should be here in about ten minutes.

"Hey, boss man," called Milosh, "tell me again about the ambulance ride."

Owen chuckled as he pulled his mind off Nadia and her reaction to the phone call. He had explained over and over again how Milosh was going to be all right, but somehow he got the impression that she didn't believe him. Whatever happened to a thing called trust? He walked back over to the bed and sat down. "Let me see." He rubbed at his chin. "First they strapped you to this board, and then they put this huge neck-brace thing around your neck. They strapped an oxygen mask on you, and then they loaded you into the 'meat wagon' like a huge sack of potatoes."

Milosh's booming laughter filled the room "What a story this will make."

Owen smiled. Everything was a story to Milosh and the rest of the family. By the time Milosh expanded it, revised it, and totally distorted it, he'd have the paramedics picking up body parts and sewing them back on. "If you promise to behave and do what the doctor says, I'll tell you what the guy who was next to you in the emergency room was screaming about."

"The one behind the yellow curtain?"

"That's the one. I was talking to his wife while you went and had all those fancy pictures taken."

Milosh's eyes widened, and his face paled. He glanced around the room, fearful of prying ears. "Is he dead?"

"Nope." Owen grinned. "They sent him home already."

Milosh was just about to ask another question when the door to the room burst open. Nadia and her mother came hurrying into the room, followed by twenty-eight members of her family. Yurik was still at the construction site getting some answers on the accident. Owen spotted Sonia cradling little Liberty in her arms and tried to refigure his math. He gave up. All he knew was, there were one hell of a lot of Kandrataviches crowding into the small hospital room. Babies were crying, the older children looked scared to death, the women were all wailing and crossing themselves, and the men were arguing back and forth between themselves in Russian. Owen shook his head and wondered how they had managed to get past the nurses' station. He worked his way over to Nadia and her mother.

He reached Nadia and pulled her into his arms. Tears were streaming down her cheeks. He tenderly wiped them away. "What are you crying for? I told you he was going to be fine." He glanced at Milosh and winked. "It's going to take more than one steel beam to do him in."

Nadia looked at her father lying in bed with his wife clinging to his hands, wailing her grief in Russian. He looked a little pale, but otherwise fine. "If he's well, why can't he come home?"

"It's called a concussion. The doctor wants to keep him overnight, just as a precaution." He pulled her back against the far wall away from the crush of people. "I don't mean this the way it's going to sound, but why did *everyone* come?" He was surprised that the staff hadn't called security yet, with all the noise everyone was making.

"They came out of respect for my father." She softly smiled at the man lying in bed consoling his grieving wife.

"Are you aware there's a rule about how many visitors each patient can have in his room at a time?"

"How would I know that?" Nadia glanced around the room. The wailing had turned into a few sniffles when the women realized that Milosh was not at heaven's gate. The men's arguing had quieted down, and only Liberty was still voicing her displeasure at having her afternoon nap disturbed. "I've only been in a hospital once, and that was to pay my final respects to my grandfather." Nadia shivered slightly and leaned closer to Owen. "He died that night in his sleep."

"I'm sorry, love." He held her close and kissed the top of her head. No wonder Milosh wanted to get out of here and the family was in such an uproar. He should have listened more closely to what she had told him the other week when Liberty was born, but it still wouldn't have changed anything. Milosh was his employee, and he had needed medical attention. There was no other place to go but a hospital. "Your father was hurt, Nadia, and I did what I thought was best for him."

"I know you did, Owen." She leaned up and kissed him on the cheek. "Thank you for taking such good care of him."

"He's a tough old boot." He chuckled softly. "But he grows on you."

Howe Cartland, the construction-site supervisor, stuck his head into the room, waving to Milosh and motioning to Owen. He acknowledged the gesture and then gazed down at Nadia. "I'll be right back." He kissed her quickly and wove his way through her family to get to the door.

Nadia frowned. Something was up. She squeezed her way through two of her aunts and kissed her father. "I'll be right back, Papa, you behave yourself." She quickly followed Owen.

She found Owen, Howe Cartland, and her uncle

Yurik, who was clasping the back of some young man's shirt, daring him to move. The young man looked scared enough to expire on the spot. All the men noticed her but continued their discussion.

"It was supposed to look like Milosh goofed while chaining the steel beam to the hoist. The beam would slip, hopefully get damaged, and you would fire Milosh for being incompetent," said Howe.

Owen turned to the red-faced man being detained by Yurik. "Want to tell your side of the story, Bill?"

"No one was supposed to get hurt."

"Tell that to Milosh," snapped Owen. "That beam broke free and was swinging straight for Jimmie Lee. If Milosh hadn't pushed Jimmie Lee aside, he would have been crushed. As it is, Milosh is lucky to be alive."

Bill appeared on the verge of tears. "But no one was supposed to get hurt." Yurik's fist tightened on the shirt, and Bill's top button dug a little deeper into his throat. "He said no one would get hurt."

"Who said?"

"Wyatt Marshall told me how to do it." He wiped his arm across the top portion of his face, leaving behind a trail of moisture and dirt. "He said no one would get hurt."

"How much did he pay you?" snapped Owen.

"Nothing." The button dug a little deeper. "He canceled my debt." The button eased up a little bit. "I owed him a couple of hundred from a card game last month. I couldn't pay."

Owen's and Nadia's gazes locked. They had both known Marshall would try something; they just hadn't expected this. "Your father's a hero," said Owen.

Nadia shrugged her shoulders. "Having an imprint of a steel beam in your skull doesn't sound like the work of a hero to me, more like that of a fool."

"Speaking of fools," said Yurik, "I go see my brother now." He pushed a frightened Bill toward Howe Cartland.

Owen shook Yurik's hand. "Thanks for all your help, Yurik. I'm sure it would have taken us a whole lot longer to get to the bottom of this without you."

Yurik cracked his knuckles and grinned at the red mark on Bill's jaw. "It's been my unadulterated pleasure."

"While you're in there, Yurik, tell Milosh what happened, and that I'll be in in a few minutes to talk to him about pressing charges."

He watched Yurik head down the hall before turning to Howe. "Watch Bill here, while I go to the nurses' station and call the police." He grasped Nadia's hand and started down the hall.

Nadia glanced at Owen sideways. "Do you have to call the police?"

"That stunt almost cost two men their lives; one of them was your father." He frowned at the commotion going on at the nurses' station. Three nurses, a doctor, two of Nadia's aunts, and an uncle were standing there arguing. He and Nadia eased in closer and listened to the dispute. The nurses wanted all but two visitors out of Milosh's room. The doctor wanted his patient to get some rest, and the aunts and uncle were doing a superb job of not understanding a single word of English.

Owen laughed and hugged Nadia tighter. "It's your family—do you want to handle this, or should I?"

Nadia sighed, smiled sweetly at the nurses and doctor, and then proceeded to blister the paint off the walls as she tore into her family in Russian.

Owen pulled a nurse aside and asked if he could borrow the phone to call the police. It seemed that the accident wasn't an accident and that his supervisor was holding the culprit in the solarium. The nurse pushed the phone across the counter without batting an eyelash.

Twenty minutes later the police arrived to haul Bill away, and Nadia had succeeded in removing everyone but her mother from Milosh's room. She glanced at the overflowing solarium and groaned. Her family were making themselves at home with the various patients who had left their rooms to see what all the commotion was about. Yelena was sitting on the floor in front of a wheelchair reading the palm of some old man in blue plaid pajamas. Volga was holding court in the corner with three old ladies, telling them the story about when some old hag put the evil eye on the entire family. A circle of patients had gathered around the babies, making childish prattle, and passing little Liberty around. One nurse looked dazed and bewildered, but Nadia couldn't tell if it was from the crowd or because Stevo was making a pass at her.

"Owen, I can't get my mother to leave," said Nadia. "She won't come home with us."

He gave her a quick hug. "I'll handle it." He walked briskly away, leaving her to deal with the other twenty-nine members of her family.

Five minutes later he was back. "It's all settled."

"She's coming?"

"Nope, she's staying too."

"In the hospital?" Nadia passed little two-year-old Tatiana back to her mother. "She can't stay in the hospital—she's not ill."

"I arranged for them to move a cot into your father's room for her. She can sleep in there for the night."

"They allow that?"

"Since he's in a private room, and she's having a very calming affect on him, they'll break the rules this once." He pulled her down the hall toward her father's room. "I also explained that he wouldn't stay unless she did."

Nadia stopped before the door. "Are you sure it's okay?"

He reached out tenderly and brushed her cheek with the back of his fingers. "Do you trust me, Nadia?"

She studied the strong curve of his jaw, the faint traces of dirt left over from the construction site, his tousled hair, and the love shining in his eyes.

How could she not trust the man she loved? He was tender, sweet, and incredibly sexy. She wanted to be his beloved more than anything else in the world. He'd earned her trust and her love weeks ago, but she hadn't returned the favor. How could she expect Owen to trust her when she held secrets? Secrets that were bound to rip them apart. Yes, she trusted Owen with her heart, her family, and her life.

She reached for his hand and brought it to her mouth. Her lips caressed its rough palm. "Yes, Owen, I do trust you."

"Stop that," said Nadia, "it tickles." She took another swing at the long weed Owen was using to tickle the bottom of her feet and missed. "You promised you would behave yourself this time."

"I am behaving myself." Owen feathered the weed over her ankle and up her slender, tan calf. "Aren't my clothes still on?"

"Amazingly, yes." She idly brushed the tips of her fingers off the strings of her guitar.

"Then that proves I'm behaving." He dug into the picnic basket sitting beside him and pulled out an apple. "Last week when I had you out here, I didn't behave, and I ended up with a sunburn on a very embarrassing part of my anatomy." His hand rubbed his bottom.

"That's what happens when you fall asleep on top of me." She crossed her legs and sat up straighter.

"Do you want to hear 'Naughty Niki' in Polish, or what?" Niki was a mischievous little spider monkey who loved getting into trouble.

Owen grinned wickedly and teased, "I'll take the 'or what.' "

Nadia felt herself start to melt under his playfulness. After all these weeks he still held the power to turn her on with just a smile, a heated look, or a word. She glanced around the secluded picnic spot. IRS and Victoria Rose were quietly munching on tall grass in the protective shade of a grove of trees. The creek was a few feet away, babbling as the cool water rushed over the rocks in its race downstream. Wildflowers dotted the small meadow, and the sun warmed her skin as well as her soul. It was their little piece of heaven they had found on the farthest corner of the Kandratavich Ranch. Nothing could touch them here. Not Wyatt Marshall and the upcoming court date. Not her disappearing music and the one last song. And most especially not the secrets she was still holding from Owen.

Her fingers stilled on the string. She didn't feel like practicing anymore today. She wanted to hold Owen and make another memory. "I thought you said you wanted to hear some foreign languages."

The palm of his hand grazed her thigh. "I do." His finger traced the line across the top of her thigh where her shorts ended. He smiled as the muscles twitched and her breath caught. "Do you know you speak in foreign words when we make love?" He removed the guitar from her hands and placed it on the blanket beside them.

"Sorry." A flush swept up her cheeks. "I sometimes get carried away and forget what language I'm using." It was halfway the truth. The other reason she spoke in different languages was that she wanted to hide her true feelings. Twice she had told Owen she loved him; both times had been in Russian, and he hadn't understood a single word she had said.

His fingers skimmed up her shorts and climbed the buttons on her blouse. "Don't be sorry." He slowly eased her back onto the blanket. "It's erotic as all hell having you whispering all those foreign-sounding words into my ear." He stroked the fullness of her lower lip with his thumb. "I can put my own meaning to those words."

She reached under his shirt and caressed the warmth of his back. "I suppose you could." It didn't matter what meaning he put to her words; nothing could compare to some of the things she had whispered to him in the dark.

"I have a story for you, love." He brushed her hair out so that it spread like dark silk across the yellow blanket. "There once was a wise old owl named Owen . . ."

"Who?"

"That's it, Nadia, play along." He kissed the second question from her lips. "There once was a wise old owl named Owen, who knew that with time, patience, and understanding he would learn the secret of all the words in the whole wide world." He kissed her again, more slowly this time. "One day a wild Gypsy rose handed him the key to unlock the secrets, and do you know what he found?"

Nadia's hands stilled. "No, Owen, what did he find?"

"Happiness, true happiness." He captured her mouth in a swift, deep kiss that held promises. "One day, Nadia, you will tell me the meaning of those words."

She pulled his head down and kissed him with everything inside her. She didn't want him to see the tears that filled her eyes. With her heart opening up a little more, she allowed the magic to carry them away to that sweet place only Owen could take them.

Owen slowed his car as he passed in front of Nadia's house, but continued down the rutted path toward the camp. With any luck maybe he wouldn't end up in the middle of the squabble between Nadia and her father. How he always ended up defending her family was a total mystery to him. He guessed it had to do with their childlike innocence. He glanced over at Milosh sitting proudly beside him in the passenger seat and grimaced at the huge ice bag he was holding over his eye. "Are you sure you don't want a doctor to take a look at that?"

"*Nyet*, I like Olenka to—how do you say?—fuzz over me."

Owen chuckled, "It's *fuss* over you."

"*Da, da,* fuss over me." He lowered the ice bag. "I thank you again, my friend, for coming to get me." He grabbed one of Owen's hands off the steering wheel and gave it a robust shake. "How many English dollars do I owe you?"

Owen barely managed to steer around a huge rut. "Many, my friend." He glanced ahead at the camp and frowned when he saw Nadia standing by the tables with her uncles. "It's not the money I'm concerned about, Milosh—it's your mule-headed daughter."

Milosh gave a hardy laugh. "*Da, da,* head like a donkey, but she has a heart like a doughnut."

Owen momentarily frowned and then smiled. "You mean cream puff, Milosh, not doughnut." He brought the car to a halt and watched as Nadia and the rest of her family started toward them. It was too late to turn back now. Hell was surely going to break out now. And by the look on Nadia's usually smiling face, he was afraid he wasn't going to go unnoticed in the battle. "She doesn't look like a cream puff right now, Milosh."

Milosh groaned, placed the ice bag back over his swollen eye, and winked at Owen. "I'll know how to handle my sweet little Nadia." He slowly opened the door and whispered, "I've been doing it for twenty-eight years; listen and learn my friend." With an extravagant moan he slowly stood up and faced his approaching family.

Owen watched the expression on Nadia's face

change from fury to concern and shook his head. He guessed the old boot knew exactly what he was doing. Interested to see how Milosh was going to get out of this one, he opened his door and joined the crowd.

"Where have you been, Papa?" asked Nadia. She shot a curious glance at Owen.

"What happened to your eye?" cried Olenka, working her way forward and removing the ice bag.

"I've been to hell in America, child," said Milosh. He smiled lovingly at his wife as she fussed and cooed over his multicolored eye.

Owen sighed as Nadia glanced at him for further clarification. So that was how Milosh was going to handle her, by letting him take the heat. "He was in jail."

Nadia looked at her father and cried, "They hit you in jail?"

"No one hit him once he was in jail, Nadia. Calm down." He didn't need her rushing off to the police station to confront the sheriff. Owen glared at the stubbornly quiet Milosh. "It seems your father went out to Wyatt Marshall's place and confronted him about putting Bill up to tampering with the equipment."

"You didn't Papa!" She paced in front of him and glared at her uncles, who were all looking at Milosh with growing respect. "You were supposed to let the courts handle it."

"I told Owen I no press those charges." He pointed at his burly chest and announced, "I am

Milosh Kandratavich, and I am a free man. I no let some man in a black dress tell me what is right and how to defend my family."

Nadia glanced at Owen. "What about the court date next month?"

"Since your father refused to press charges, my company will. Wyatt Marshall has to pay for what he did. Someone could have been killed, and I don't want him thinking he's free to pull anything else. Next time someone might not be so lucky."

"Great." Nadia sighed. She glared at her father. "I gather that Marshall was the one who gave you that lovely eye."

"He only hit me once," snapped Milosh, "and that's because the man is a coward. He blindsided me when I wasn't looking."

"So why were you in jail?"

"Because I hit him back."

Nadia glanced back at Owen. "They jail people in America for defending themselves?"

"Well, no," admitted Owen. "Your father is a man in excellent physical condition, while Marshall has . . . let himself go to seed, shall we say." Owen glanced at Milosh and tried to hide the respect he felt for the old boot. "It seems your father laid him out pretty good."

"So where do you fit into all of this?" asked Nadia. "Don't tell me you drove him out to Marshall's."

"Of course not. I didn't know anything about it until I received his phone call from jail. It seems your father thought I was the best candidate to come and bail him out."

Nadia slowly turned to her father, raised a finger, and poked him in the chest. "How could—"

Milosh brushed aside her finger and moved away from the fender on Owen's car. He clapped his hands twice and bellowed, "Family, I have an announcement to make." Silence fell across the masses. "My best American friend, Owen, has done me and my family a great service by coming to my rescue and standing up for me. I owe him a debt of gratitude, and I finally figured out how to pay him." He glanced around the crowd until he was positive he had everyone's attention. "I, Milosh Zurka Kandratavich, give you, Owen, one of my greatest treasures, my daughter Nadia Katrinka's hand in marriage."

Owen's mouth fell open to his knees.

Nadia didn't look at Owen but continued to stare at her father as if she had never seen him before. A tide of red swept up her face as she quietly said something to her parents in Russian. With each sentence her voice rose and her words came faster. Her arms punctuated her words, and the rest of the family took a few safe steps backward. Milosh continued to grin as her words became more vocal and rushed. She finished her reprimand in a fury, placed both hands on her hips, and glared threateningly at her father.

Owen didn't like the smile lurking on Milosh's face or the dangerous shade of red blotching Nadia's cheeks. Most of her relatives thought the whole thing was amazingly funny. Why wasn't she going along with the obvious joke? He decided to try to appeal to Nadia's sense of humor. "I gather that was a no."

Her response, in Russian, came back fast and furious. She stamped her foot and shook her tiny fist, and without comprehending a word, Owen knew she had to be cursing him to a slow, painful death. In a swirl of dust she stomped off, leaving the group staring after her in wonder.

Owen moved to follow her and was stopped by Milosh's hand. "If you value your life, let her cool down first, my best friend in America."

"I'm your only friend in America, Milosh." Owen shook off his hand and stared at the hill Nadia had just climbed. She was not heading home. She was walking toward the creek. "Want to explain to me why Nadia reacted so furiously to a joke?" He glanced at Milosh and frowned. "Please tell me it *was* a joke."

"*Da da*, it was a joke," said Milosh. "I told Nadia long ago that she may marry for love." He glanced at his wife and gently smiled. "We want all our children to have what we have."

"So what upset her?"

"She remembers too much." Milosh sadly shook his head. "She remembers friends being forced to marry men they didn't love and sometimes men they did not know. The practice of arranged marriages still goes on in many Gypsy tribes."

Owen ran his fingers through his hair. "So why in the hell would you even joke about such a thing?"

Milosh smiled proudly. "To stop her from lecturing me about getting thrown in jail."

Owen muttered a silent oath.

"Don't look so down, my friend," said Milosh as he smacked Owen across the back. "Things are splendid."

"How can you say that?"

"Did you not notice the way my daughter attacked my plan?"

"How could I miss it? She was mad as hell."

"*Da, da*, that is good." Milosh crossed his arms and beamed. "If she'd laughed it off, that is bad. It shows she has no feelings for you. But since she is"—he made a sour face—"mad as hell, it shows she has many feelings for you, my American friend."

Owen rubbed his chin for a moment. "I wouldn't give you a plug nickel for her feelings right about now."

"What is this plug nickel?"

"It's a . . . never mind, Milosh." He started to cross the camp to follow Nadia. "Milosh, my best Gypsy friend, do me a huge favor?"

"Name it, and it shall be yours."

Owen continued to walk and called over his shoulder, "Next time you're in jail, don't call me."

TEN

Owen found Nadia sitting alone under a tree throwing tiny pebbles into the creek. He slowly made his way under the branches and sat down beside her. "Is it safe to sit here?"

"It's a free country." She didn't bother to look at him but continued to pluck up little pebbles from in front of her and pitch them into the clear water.

"The country might be free, but you own the ranch."

"I might own two thirds of the ranch, but *Prescott* Mortgage Company owns the other third." She pitched the next stone with a little more force. "Who's to say you're not sitting on the *Prescott* third?"

"For the last time, Nadia, I don't have anything to do with the mortgage company."

"It bears your name."

He sighed heavily, leaned back onto his elbows, and crossed his long legs. "Why do you want to pick a fight with me?" He gazed at the stubborn tilt of her chin. "Is it because your father called me instead of you to come bail him out of jail? How about it's because your father told a tasteless joke? They both sound like real good reasons to take it all out on me."

Nadia wrapped her arms around her knees and rested her chin on top. "I'm sorry, Owen, it's not you I'm mad at." She stared at the creek. "I'm not even mad at my father. He didn't do anything I hadn't expected him to do." She owed Owen some of the truth at least. "I'm mad at myself."

"For what?"

"Burning bridges." A stone landed in the middle of the creek with a resounding plop.

Owen stared at her serious-looking expression. "What bridges did you burn, Nadia?"

"Nothing major." She gave a sad little chuckle. "They were only the most important ones." *The ones that lead to happiness and love.*

"Want to tell me about them?"

"Not particularly."

"I thought you trusted me?"

Nadia cringed at the pain in Owen's question. She held his hurt gaze. "I do trust you, Owen."

"But not enough to share your secrets?"

"Trust has nothing to do with it." She looked away as tears filled her eyes. "My secrets are my shame. They are mine alone to bear."

He gently cupped her chin and forced her to face

him. His smile was full of tenderness and love. "Some people say my shoulders are mighty broad."

She glanced at the width of his shoulders stretching the tan cotton shirt. "They are right, Owen. Your shoulders are beautifully formed." She remembered clutching at them as if they were the only solid thing left on earth as Owen took her to the stars night after night.

He softly chuckled. "You misunderstood, Nadia. I wasn't referring to their shape, but to their ability. When a person has broad shoulders, it means that he's willing to shoulder other people's problems." The tips of his fingers brushed her lower lip. "You know, help with the load."

"Why should you want to carry my problems? I made them, not you."

His fingers stopped, and his relaxed expression vanished. "When you love someone, Nadia, you share the burden." His gaze traveled over every inch of her face. "I love you, Nadia." His lips followed the same path. Kisses feathered over her forehead, teasing her silky, long lashes and the tip of her upturned nose. "Let me share the burden." His mouth captured the lone, salty tear sliding down her pale cheek.

"I'm afraid."

"Of what?"

She reached up and stroked his slightly stubbled jaw. It had been hours since his last encounter with a razor. At this moment she should be the happiest woman in America, but she wasn't. The man she loved had just said the most precious words a man could say to a woman, and she couldn't return them. She couldn't declare her love and still withhold secrets from him. Owen deserved better than that. He deserved better than a woman who was too darn selfish to give him up. "I'm afraid of losing you."

He smiled and rubbed his abrasive jaw against the palm of her hand. "You won't lose me."

"How can you be so sure? You don't know the past."

"Is there a husband that I don't know about?" He locked gazes with her and ran the tip of his tongue over the base of her thumb.

"*Married!* You think I'm married!" She tried to yank her hand out of his grasp. "You don't think very highly of me, do you?"

He chuckled and continued to tease her fingers. "I happen to think very highly of you, love. It's you who have a problem with self-esteem." He nipped at the tip of her finger. "I just mentioned the worst thing I could think of. I figured as long as you aren't married to someone else, anything else will be a piece of cake." He nibbled on the next fingertip. "You aren't wanted by the police or anything?"

"Don't be ridiculous." He was hitting too close to home. The police had interviewed her for hours, for days, and for weeks before they finally got it through their heads that she didn't know anything. She had only been a front, very well paid for her ignorance.

"Well, if you aren't married and you aren't wanted by the police, I don't see what the problem is."

"What about the past?"

"What about it?" His lips traveled over her delicate wrist and up to the sensitive skin on the inside of her elbow.

"Don't you care about what I might have done?" She shivered as his lips wandered higher across the smoothness of her shoulder to toy with the collar of her blouse.

Owen raised his head. "I'll be truthful with you, love. I'm naturally curious to know what's made you feel so bad about yourself, but whatever it was, it won't change how I feel about you." He gently pushed her back onto the sweet-smelling grass behind her. "I don't care about your past, Nadia." He leaned over her and brushed a dark curl away from her mouth. "It's your future I'm concerned about." His face lowered, and his breath feathered across her waiting lips. "Our future, Nadia, yours and mine together."

"But . . ."

He placed a finger to her lips. "In America *but* means the end, so this discussion is finished." His lips replaced his finger with a tender kiss. "If one day you want to tell me about the past, fine. I will listen with an open mind, but I will not judge you, love. The past is not important."

Nadia surrendered to the sweet, seductive lure of his lips. He was offering another day of paradise, and she grabbed onto it with both hands. He was wrong.

The past did matter. It had made her stronger, more independent, and it had stolen her innocence. It had made her who she was today, and one day Owen would want to know and she would have to tell him. That day paradise would be taken away from her.

She reached up and tightened her hold around Owen's neck. She felt his answering response and melted. He loved her! Her kiss became more heated, more desperate. She had to hold on to paradise for as long as she could.

Nadia slowly hung up the phone and glanced at Owen, who was sitting in the kitchen on the wobbly chair stirring his coffee, desperately trying to pretend he hadn't been eavesdropping. She tried to muster a smile, failed miserably, walked over to the screen door, and stared out toward the barn. The fence had all been repaired and was sporting a brand-new coat of white paint. Yesterday one of her brothers had spent the entire day mowing grass and straightening up the yard, and Rupa had fixed the hayloft door so that it wasn't hanging by one hinge anymore. The Kandratavich Ranch was improving by leaps and bounds. Even IRS and Victoria Rose were prancing proudly around the corral as though they were the ones who had done the work. What were they going to do if she couldn't meet the payments on the ranch? They could lose it all.

Owen silently came up behind her and wrapped

an arm around her waist. He tucked her head under his chin and studied the view she was seeing. "Want to tell me about it?"

"That was the recording studio." She leaned back and allowed his warmth and strength to surround her. "They moved the recording schedule up three weeks." She closed her eyes and concentrated on the sound of the light summer breeze and the buzzing of a bee by the wisteria bush climbing the side of the porch. Normal, everyday summer sounds drifted in through the screen. She could hear everything, including Owen's soft breathing, but she couldn't detect one note. Her music hadn't returned, and time was running out. "I have less than a month to finish writing the songs."

His arms tightened slightly, and he kissed the top of her head. "It will come, Nadia. Give it a chance."

"I've given it over a month, and still nothing but silence. All the work on the other songs is complete. I'm ready to record them in six languages. The only thing stopping me is one last song. The whole thing is worthless without that song." She smacked the metal frame of the screen door with the palm of her hand. "It's my punishment, Owen, for being greedy."

He tried not to chuckle and ended up choking. When he could breathe again, he muttered in astonishment, "You, greedy?" She was the most unselfish person he had ever met. He would have given her the moon or the stars if she asked. She had no living-room furniture, yet she had gone out and spent her share of the catering money on a bureau for her new little niece, Liberty.

"I wanted it all."

"All of what?" He had no idea what she wanted, but he'd make sure she got it.

"I wanted my family out of Europe. I wanted a nice place where we could all live in peace and freedom."

"That's not greed, Nadia, that's love." He turned her in his arms so he could look at her. "Don't you see? You have all that."

"I sacrificed everything I believed in to get them out, Owen." She looked away from him. "It's not something I'm proud of, but I would do it again. As for the ranch . . ." She shrugged her shoulders, "I borrowed against a dream. One that is now on the brink of failure. If the album is scrapped, I lose the first true home my family has ever known."

"You won't lose the ranch, love." He tilted up her chin and brushed her mouth with a soft kiss. "I won't let you lose it."

"I won't accept your help, Owen."

"Why not?" he demanded. "I'm fully capable of helping you out of this tight situation. You can repay me when your music returns and you can record the album."

"*Money! You're offering me money?*" She stepped out of his arms. In the space of a moment he had reduced everything they had to dollars and cents. She had sold herself once, and she wouldn't do it again. She would rather see her family living out of the *vardos* and traveling the back roads of America before she would allow Owen to put a price on their love.

"I'm offering you a chance to save the dream, Nadia."

"No, Owen. You're offering to buy it." She stepped away from him and headed for the coffeepot Owen had bought after their first week together. "Do you really want to do something for me?"

"You know I do."

"Then help me find my music."

"I might not be able to find your music, Nadia." A playful smile teased the corner of his mouth. "But I can show you where to find other people's music."

Nadia glanced around the crowded store with utter delight. Records, tapes, and CDs were jammed into every available inch of space from floor to ceiling. An old Glenn Miller number was blaring out of a set of speakers on either side of the door. Crates of dusty record jackets were squeezed under overloaded tables that sagged from the weight of tapes and albums. Everywhere she looked, there was music. There were classical and opera, along with country and western, a touch of jazz, rhythm and blues, and rock. Everything was mixed helter-skelter. She had found heaven, and it was called Paul's Music Emporium. "Owen, how on earth did you ever find this place?"

Owen started to lean against a table but thought better of it. The table didn't look as if it could withstand the pile of records already heaped on it, never mind his added weight. "I stumbled onto it about five years ago." He smiled as Nadia slowly spun in circles. She had no idea where to start. Paul's had that effect on first-time customers. It had taken him three trips to realize he could never search through all the stacks, so every time he stopped, he started in on a different area of the store, unearthing ageless treasures. After five years over half his extensive music collection had come from Paul's. "The secret to finding anything is to pick a spot and start going through it."

"Isn't there any kind of order?" Her fingers flipped through a stack of albums. Alice Cooper was mixed with Mozart and Willie Nelson.

"I think there was at one time," chuckled Owen, "but that was long before I ever walked through the door."

"Are you complaining again, rich boy?" snarled a big, burly man behind Owen.

Owen spun around and shook the man's hand. "Paul, you old snake, I see you still like to go sneaking around." Paul flashed a nearly toothless grin that spoke of too many fistfights, and shook his hand harder. "Paul, I would like you to meet a very special lady, Nadia Kandratavich." He turned to her. "Nadia, this is the owner, Paul."

Nadia glanced at the man and hid her surprise. She had expected someone a little different to be running the music store. Paul stood six foot four and had a build designed for Mack trucks. He wore torn jeans and a black Harley-Davidson T-shirt that was stretched to its limits. A thick chrome chain served as his belt, and black motorcycle boots boasted not only age but the evidence that they had kicked in a few doors in their youth. Paul's nearly white hair hung halfway down his back in a ponytail, and his thick beard covered most of the golden eagle printed on his shirt. She held out her hand and grinned at the three golden hoops he wore in his right ear. "Hello, Paul, it is indeed my pleasure to meet the person responsible for all of this." She waved her hand around the room.

Paul raised her hand and lightly pressed a kiss to the back of her fingers. "I now understand why Owen hasn't dropped by in the past couple of months."

Nadia glanced at Owen and willed the blush rising in her cheeks down. "I can assure you, sir, that had I known about this place sooner, we would have been here." She moved to another stack of albums and started to dig through it.

Owen shook his head as Paul chuckled. "You might think it's funny now, but in six hours when you close for the day and we still can't get her out of here, then what will you do?" asked Owen.

Paul leaned against the counter and admired the view of Nadia bending over the table. "Stay open late, I guess."

Owen moved closer to Nadia to see what album

had caught her attention. "Then I suggest you go call your wife and five kids now and tell them you'll be late for dinner."

Two hours later Owen tapped Nadia on her shoulder. "Lunch is ready."

"Lunch?" She brushed a hand across her eyes and blinked.

"It's after one, love." He waved his hand in the direction of the counter where Paul was in the process of moving off a stack of records and tapes to make room for their lunch. "I figured since it looked like I would have to drag you kicking and screaming from that stack of old records, I'd pick up something for us to eat."

She glanced at the two paper bags sitting on the spot Paul had just cleared. "You went out?"

Owen groaned and clutched at his chest. "Why don't you just cut out my heart with a knife—it would be less painful."

Nadia flushed as Paul's booming laughter filled the shop. She wiped her dirty hands on the side of her jeans. "Well, you could have at least told me." She carefully picked up the couple of albums she had unearthed from the masses.

"I did, Nadia. I told you I was running next door to pick up some sandwiches and soda, and do you know what you told me?"

She lovingly dusted off each album with a rag

Paul had handed her. She really couldn't afford to buy the albums, but she was willing to give up eating for the week to own them. Some things were just more important than food. She glanced at Owen. "If I don't remember you leaving, how do you expect me to remember what I said?"

"You told me to drive carefully." He pulled a pile of sandwiches and a large bag of chips from the paper sack.

"So?" She glanced at her hands and frowned. They were filthy from rummaging through dusty stacks of albums. "Paul, do you have a place where I can wash up?"

He jerked his thumb toward a beaded curtain. "In the back there's a washroom. Help yourself."

"Thanks." She gently set the albums aside. "Don't let anyone touch these," she said, and disappeared through the curtain.

Paul shook his head and grinned at his friend. "She has it bad, doesn't she?"

He tossed Paul a soda. "When the music bug bit her, it didn't let go." Owen tore into the bag of chips and popped the top on his soda can. "She's a singer, you know."

"Really? Who's she with?" Paul grabbed a handful of chips.

"No one, she's solo. She's recording a children's album next month in six languages."

Paul's bushy white eyebrows met his hairline. "Impressive! What did she do before that?"

"She sang in some nightclub in New York. Very high class with big bucks."

Paul thoughtfully studied Nadia as she came through the beaded curtain and joined them. He pulled out a stool from behind the counter for her. "Owen tells me you sang up in New York. Which club did you sing at?"

Nadia concentrated on unwrapping her sandwich. "It was some local joint—you probably never heard of it." She smiled at Owen as he handed her a soda. "You ever been to New York, Paul?"

"I get up there a couple times a year. My parents live up there, and they like to have the grandkids visit." He took a bite out of his sandwich and frowned at Nadia as she nervously picked at her lunch. "You look awfully familiar. Have you ever performed on television?"

"No, I've never *performed* on television." Having reporters jam cameras into her face and microphones under her nose just to boost the six-o'clock news ratings didn't count as performing. She took a hasty bite out of her sandwich. It could have tasted like one of her father's old work boots for all she cared. Paul had recognized her! Any minute now he was going to match her face with the front-page headlines that had tantalized the citizens of New York for months. It didn't matter was that half of what had been printed was untrue and the other 50 percent pure speculation. What did matter was that some snot-nosed reporter had christened her the "Manhattan Mistress" and she had been cast as a leading player in a high-profile drama.

"I could swear I've seen you somewhere," muttered Paul.

Owen studied the lack of color in Nadia's cheeks. "They say every person has a double."

"That must be it," said Paul. He looked at Nadia and grinned. "Ever been to California?"

"The land of surfer dudes, Hollywood, and earthquakes?" Nadia shook her head and relaxed her shoulders. "Afraid not." Hoping to keep Paul away from New York, she asked, "Ever been to Budapest?"

"Nope. I hoofed it through Albuquerque once when my hog died."

Nadia glanced at Owen in confusion. Why was Paul talking about farm animals?

Owen laughed at the expression on Nadia's face. "Paul said he had to walk through the city of Albuquerque, New Mexico, once when his motorcycle died."

Nadia returned Paul's grin. "I've never been to New Mexico, and I have never ridden a pig."

Paul groaned and clutched his chest as Owen's boisterous laughter filled the tiny shop. "Nadia, love," said Owen choking, as he regained his breath. "If you plan on leaving here with those albums and your life, never refer to Paul's one true love as a pig—it's a hog, love, a hog." He crumbled up the empty wrappings from their sandwiches and tossed them into the wastebasket under the counter.

Nadia pitched her empty soda can into the recycle basket and headed back to the corner of the shop where she had been shuffling through old albums. She purposely turned her back toward Paul and kept her head down. If she insisted on leaving now after being totally engrossed in the shop all morning, Owen would know something was wrong. It had been bad enough that he'd stared at her funny all during lunch; she didn't need to add any more suspicion. With any luck Paul would forget all about where he had seen her before if she stayed out of his sight.

Paul sat on the stool thoughtfully staring at the back of Nadia's head and pulling on his bead. Owen stood by a stack of records and glanced between Nadia and Paul. A deep frown pulled at his mouth.

Nadia squeezed in between two tables and reached for a stack of albums covered with dust. With a swipe of a rag she sent dust bunnies flying in every direction and uncovered a Pat Boone album. She tried to smile at the handsome young man gracing the cover of the album in her hand and failed. The magic of searching through this enchanted treasure trove had vanished. All she wanted to do was get away from Paul before he figured out where he had seen her.

"I don't know, Owen, maybe we should just go to my place," said Nadia. She glanced at Owen's impressive home as they pulled into the driveway. She had never felt comfortable here and had made up countless excuses to avoid spending the night in Owen's king-size bed with its designer sheets. He always slept in her crowded double bed with its old sheets.

"You're the one who mentioned wanting to hear those records on my stereo system."

"That's because you didn't buy your stereo during a blue-light special." She reached for the bag containing the dozen albums she had purchased from Paul. The headache she had used as an excuse to leave the shop early had really developed during the fifty-minute ride home from Asheville. She opened the car door and frowned at the stately mansion. "Won't we be disturbing your aunt?"

"Aunt Verna and a couple of her lady friends went to Cape Hatteras for a few days." He came around to the front of the car and took her elbow. "So we have the entire house to ourselves."

"What about Sebastian and Milly?" She glanced at the huge ceramic urns on either side of the front door. They were overflowing with a kaleidoscope of colorful blooms. Each perfect flower looked fresh and color-coordinated for that particular spot. Not one petal appeared wilted or blemished. They were picture-perfect, and they represented Owen's life. He had a flawless home, a perfectly wonderful aunt, an ideal career, and an upstanding reputation in the community. Everything in his life was perfect—except her.

Owen chuckled at her fierce expression. "What did those flowers ever do to you?" He pulled her inside the cool foyer. "Is your headache that bad?"

He took the bag from her hands and placed it on the table beside the door.

Nadia rubbed her temples. "Do you have any aspirin?"

"I'll get it, sir," drawled Sebastian.

Nadia glanced at the butler, who had entered the hall without her knowledge. "I can get them, Sebastian, if you can tell me where they are." She felt like a bigger phony having Sebastian wait on her.

Owen continued to look at Nadia for a moment. "There is a bottle of aspirin in the powder room off my office, Nadia."

"Thanks." She gave Sebastian a small smile before disappearing down the hall toward Owen's office.

She returned a few minutes later and found Owen standing in front of his stereo placing one of her records on the turntable. A tray of cool drinks and delicate little cakes sat on the coffee table in front of the couch. "I see Sebastian's been busy."

"I got that for us." He pushed a few buttons, and the first strains of a Mozart concerto filled the room. "I gave Sebastian and Milly the night off."

"Why?"

"For some reason they seem to make you nervous." He sat down on the couch and picked up his glass. "Want to tell me why?"

"They don't make me nervous, really." She toyed with one of the throw pillows. "It's just that I'm not the type who likes to be waited on."

"Getting you a couple of aspirin is hardly the same thing as having Sebastian at your beck and call."

"I bet if I spill this drink, he'd be in here cleaning up before the ice cubes had a chance to melt into the carpet."

"Tonight you will have to clean up your own mess. He's already gone for the evening." Owen replaced his drink on the tray and stood up. "Come here, I have something I want you to see."

Nadia took his hand and rose from the couch. "Are you going to try to seduce me?"

He shook his head as he led her out of the room and into the hall. "How's the headache?"

Had it really only been nine hours since they'd made love? How was she ever going to survive letting him go? "It's practically gone."

"Good." He gently tugged her toward the massive curved stairway.

"Does that mean you are going to seduce me?"

"Let me know when it's all gone, and we'll discuss it." He started to climb the oak stairs. "Right now I have someone I want you to see."

"I thought you said we have the house to ourselves?"

"We do." He hauled her up the massive stairs, past gilded framed portraits of his ancestors. He didn't spare her a moment to study the paintings but continued up until they reached the upstairs hall. He stopped in front of a huge portrait lit by discreetly placed track lighting. "I want you to see my great-

great-grandmother, Morning Eyes Prescott."

Nadia studied the painting with wonder. It wasn't like the other stuffy portraits adorning the stairway. The young Indian maiden sitting by a stream was lovely and as graceful as the natural beauty surrounding her. She was dressed in a buckskin dress decorated with fringe and colorful beads. Her hair was as black as midnight and braided, and her cheekbones were high and proud, but it was her eyes that captured Nadia's attention. They were as blue as the morning skies. "Your great-great-grandmother was an American Indian?"

"Half American Indian. Her mother was Cherokee, but her unknown father was white. When she was five, her mother died, leaving her in the care of the local spinster schoolmarm, who raised her as her own. Jeremiah Prescott fell in love with her the instant he laid eyes on her. They were married three weeks after they met."

"That's a wonderful story." She smiled at the painting. Morning Eyes lived every woman's fantasy: to be swept off her feet by the man she loved.

"It wasn't that wonderful in the beginning. The whole town opposed the marriage of their Civil War hero, General Jeremiah Prescott, to—as Morning Eyes put it in her diary—some half-breed trash."

"That's terrible," cried Nadia.

"I agree." Owen leaned against the wall and studied the living, breathing woman in front of him. "Not only did Morning Eyes have the snobbery of the whole town to deal with, she now had servants to do her bidding."

Nadia glanced between Owen and the painting. "What did she do?"

"First she pleaded with Jeremiah to let half the staff go, but he refused."

"Why? It seems like a reasonable request to me."

"Because they had nowhere to go. It was right after the Civil War, and money was scarce for everyone. With their limited skills, no one would hire them. At least here they had a roof over their heads, food in their bellies, and a few coins in their pockets."

"So what happened?"

"By the time Morning Eyes gave birth to their seventh child, she had doubled the size of the staff." He chuckled and grinned at the portrait of his great-great-grandmother. "It seems through the years she hired every stray that came to the back door asking for work or a handout. Rumor also had it that the Prescotts' servants were the highest paid in the state."

Nadia glanced at the portrait and smiled. "Your ancestor was one smart woman."

"That she was." He moved away from the wall. "She was also kindhearted and generous." He reached out and brushed his fingers across her smooth cheek and into her hair. He wrapped a curl around his hand. "You remind me of her."

"Me?" laughed Nadia, shaking her head and causing the curls to tighten around his fist.

"Prescott men have a tradition of picking the finest wives." He eased his fingers out of her hair and slipped them around to the back of her neck. "If I promise to give Sebastian and Milly a raise, will you marry me, Nadia?"

Her gaze flew to his face. He was serious! Oh, Lord, what was she going to do? "I . . . I . . ." She swallowed the lump lodged in her throat and tried to think of something to say. "I . . ."

Owen smiled gently. "You're stuttering, love."

"I . . ." She ran her sweaty palms down the sides of her jeans as her mind whirled. She should say no, she should say yes. She should tell Owen everything and give him a chance to take back the question. She should keep her mouth shut and pray that he would never find out about her past. Desperate for time, she stuttered, "I don't know what to say."

"Say yes." He pulled her closer and teased her mouth with a quick kiss. "How's the headache now?"

She blinked in confusion. "What headache?"

He laughed and was about to pick her up, when the shrilling of the phone stopped him. He glared playfully down at her. "If Sebastian was here, he would get that."

She glanced down the hall when the phone rang again. "It could be important."

"It also could be someone selling cemetery plots." He tapped her on the nose. "Don't you move." He headed down the hall toward the nearest telephone. "We'll continue this discussion as soon as I return."

He took another step and grinned over his shoulder at her. "And I will be expecting an answer."

Nadia watched as he disappeared into one of the rooms. She turned and faced the portrait of Morning Eyes. Nadia frowned at the silent woman sitting so serenely under the tree by the creek. *Was your and Jeremiah's love strong enough to overcome the scorn of the town along with the differences in your backgrounds?* Nadia remembered Owen saying Morning Eyes had given birth to seven children. *Silly question.*

She stood in the middle of the hallway and felt the echoes of happiness that had filled the house over the years. Children had run down these stairs, and a mischievous boy or two must have slid down the oak banister—much to his mother's dismay, or perhaps delight.

Morning Eyes, whose only crime was to be born on the wrong side of the blanket, would have understood her dilemma. Should she save Owen any future pain and break his heart now by telling him she couldn't marry him? Or did she have Morning Eyes's strength to face the knowledge that sometimes love doesn't give you a choice?

Nadia squared her shoulders and looked solemnly at Morning Eyes. She was going to tell Owen the truth about her past, and if he was still willing to marry her, she'd jump so fast at the chance, it would seem indecent.

"Nadia?"

She quickly turned around, and the smile slid

from her face. He was giving her a very curious look. "What's wrong?"

"That was your mother on the phone." He grimaced as she paled. "It seems we have a big problem." He ran his fingers through his hair and around the inside collar of his shirt. "A real big problem."

"What's that?"

"The town's in a complete uproar, and they're after blood."

Nadia closed her eyes and asked, "What did my family do this time?"

"Your brother Nikita has run off with the mayor's daughter."

ELEVEN

"But, Officer, my parents have already told you Nikita isn't here!" shouted Nadia. The ruckus in the camp was making it hard for any one person to be heard above the noise. Not only had the sheriff and both of his deputies showed up at the camp, but they had brought along half the town, including the furious mayor and his wailing wife. From all indications sweet Anna Leigh, the missing daughter, was twenty-two years old. Surely old enough to know her own mind. The way the mayor was reacting, you would think Nikita had robbed the cradle. "Even if he and Anna Leigh were here, there is nothing you can do about it. Both are consenting adults."

Owen groaned as the mayor's wife let out a wail that was surely designed to wake the dead and leave him deaf. He moved closer to Nadia and whispered, "Maybe you can have your mother check to see if Nikita took any of his belongings."

Nadia glanced at her mother and said something

in Russian. Olenka hurried toward the mobile home where Nikita kept most of his belongings. She shook her head at the confusion reigning throughout the camp. Some of the town's menfolk were trying to question her family, who had reverted back to their favorite trick. They all pretended not to understand a single word of English. If any of the townspeople had spent the time to get to know them during the past months, they would know that all of the Kandrataviches understood and spoke English. "This is ridiculous, Owen. They are obviously miles away by now."

"I know, love." He pulled her into his arms and held her close. "This is not exactly how I planned on spending my evening."

She grinned up at him. "Do tell."

"I had something a little less crowded in mind." He toyed with a dark curl lying against her shoulder. "You never did answer my question."

Nadia was saved from answering him by her mother's appearance next to them. She spoke in rapid Russian and gestured wildly with her hands. Nadia sighed and looked at the sheriff, who was waiting for an answer. "My mother says that Nikita's stuff is gone."

"Thank your mother for looking," said the sheriff.

The mayor poked his pudgy finger into the sheriff's chest. "Evan, do something," snapped the mayor, "and do it now."

"What precisely would you like me to do? Haul the entire family in for questioning?"

The mayor's wife wailed more loudly, and the mayor turned a bright red. "I don't care what you have to do, *Sheriff*, we want our little Anna Leigh back right this minute."

"Face it, *Mayor*, your little daughter, your over-the-age-of-consent daughter, has taken it upon herself to leave for places unknown with Nikita Kandratavich, and there's nothing you can do about it."

"He kidnapped her!" shouted the mayor. "That's a federal offense."

"Kidnap victims don't pack suitcases and leave notes to their parents telling them not to worry because they have found love and happiness in the arms of Nikita." The sheriff crossed his arms and glared at the balding mayor. "I only agreed to come out here so you wouldn't take it into your head to lynch the poor boy if he and Anna Leigh were here."

"I'll have your badge for this!" shouted the mayor above his wife's renewed weeping.

"None of your women are safe," someone yelled above the commotion.

Owen gently pushed Nadia aside and stepped forward. Under his breath he muttered, "Wyatt Marshall."

"Lock your doors and hide your women. They're all liars and thieves!" shouted Wyatt. "First they cheated at cards and took my prized mare, Victoria

Rose. Then they tried to blame it on me for some old man's incompetence."

Someone shouted, "Let's ship them all back from where they came."

"Yeah, who needs their kind here!" cried another angry voice.

Owen ignored the voices and took a few more threatening steps toward the red-faced Wyatt. The man looked as though he'd been on a weeks-long drinking binge. "Shut your mouth, Wyatt. No one is interested in hearing what twenty-year-old Scotch has to say."

Wyatt took a staggering step closer to Owen. "Well, lookie here, if it ain't Mr. Defender of the Downtrodden. Hire any more thieves lately?" Silence filled the camp.

"I'm warning you, Wyatt," growled Owen.

"I'm amazed you can talk, Prescott." Wyatt glared at Nadia. "I figured it must be pretty hard with your nose buried in that tramp's skirt . . ."

Owen's fist made a bone-crunching thud as it connected with Wyatt's jaw. The man's eyes rolled into the back of their sockets as he crumpled to the ground. Owen stared down at the pile of dirty laundry and the drunken man inside it and shuddered. His gaze shifted to his throbbing fist as he muttered to himself, "I hit him!"

Milosh threw his arm around Owen's shoulder and stared down at the unconscious man. "You did good, my friend." Not caring who heard him speak, he asked in English, "We string him up now?"

"No, Milosh. We let the law handle it." He glanced at the sheriff standing beside him. "Evan, will you please lock him up until he sleeps it off." He grimaced as he flexed his fingers.

Evan tried to hide a smirk. "That's a wicked right you have there, Owen." He motioned for his two deputies.

Owen glanced at Nadia and silently held out his hand. She moved forward and tenderly grasped it. He gave it a little squeeze and glanced around at the crowd. The mayor was staring at Wyatt's crumpled body like a fish. His eyes were bugging out of his head, and his mouth kept opening and closing without saying a word. His wife finally stopped her wailing, but she looked to be in shock now. The few men from town appeared finally to comprehend that Milosh had spoken in fluent English and had understood every insulting word Wyatt had yelled. Owen sighed and tightened his grip on Nadia's hand.

"Today I am not proud to be an American," he told the crowd. "You all came here with prejudice and misunderstanding in your hearts against an entire race of people you know nothing about. Every one of you had ancestors who came to this great country and suffered the same prejudice you have shown today. Haven't we learned anything in the past three hundred years? Where is this great southern hospitality everyone is always talking about? It hasn't been in evidence since the Kandrataviches moved here. They might do things a little bit differently than we do, but who are we to say *their* way is wrong?

"Every one of you lost money to Wyatt and had to pay up. But when he lost Victoria Rose in a fair card game, he cries foul." Owen glanced at Milosh. "Every one of you know Eugene's boy Jimmie Lee. If it weren't for Milosh here risking his own life, Jimmie Lee wouldn't be with us today. And how do we repay this family? By following their children through our stores as if they were a pack of thieves ready to pick our shelves clean. By refusing to hire them for jobs they are probably overqualified to do." He pinned a tall, lean man with a glare. "Al, you've been advertising for months for a mechanic, but when Zanko arrived on your doorstep, you told him the job was filled. Chris"—Owen looked at another man—"what about that part-time job you have open at the feed mill?"

Owen gave them a minute to digest the facts before turning to the mayor. "Ellis, I've known you my entire life. You didn't come here looking for your daughter; you came here to exert your power over people. There was no law broken. Your daughter is old enough to make her own decisions. Did it ever occur to you that maybe the Kandrataviches are worried about their son? He's only been in this country for six months. Maybe they're wondering what kind of daughter you raised who would lure their baby away from them and out into a world he knows nothing about." Owen shook his head with sadness. "Maybe if you had come as a father and talked to them as parents, you could have figured out where the young lovers had gone. As it is, precious hours have been wasted."

He started to pull Nadia away from the silent crowd. "As much as I love your family, I don't want to handle any more of their problems tonight."

Nadia glanced at her family, the sheriff, and the mayor. Owen had done a superb job of handling the latest Kandratavich crisis. "I think it's safe for us to leave."

He walked over to where he had parked his car an hour ago and opened the passenger door for her. "What are the chances that we won't be disturbed again?"

She glanced at the dispersing crowd and saw the mayor shake hands with her father. The other men from town were talking to some members of her family, and the deputies were placing Wyatt in the backseat of a patrol car. One of her little cousins climbed into the front seat of the patrol car and hit the siren switch. A smile teased her mouth. "I think the odds are in our favor."

"Great!" Owen shut her door and hurried around to the driver's side. "We're going back to my place."

"Can we please go to my house, Owen?" She

glanced across the seat at him. "There's something very important I have to show you."

He started the car. "Don't tell me you have portraits of your ancestors too."

"No, something more revealing." She glanced down at her hands trembling in her lap. "I want you to see my past."

Nadia cracked an ice-cube tray and placed a couple of cubes in a clean dish towel. She walked over to Owen and positioned the makeshift ice pack over his right hand. "I don't think anything's broken. It's just swollen."

He wiggled his fingers. They were a little sore, but he had full movement. "I'm sorry, Nadia. I don't usually go around punching people." He flexed his fingers again. "In fact that was the first time I ever hit someone that wasn't in self-defense."

She started to pull the fixings for sandwiches out of the refrigerator and placed them on the table. "He was asking for it." She took down a couple of plates and began cutting thick slices of ham. "I hope sandwiches are okay." She glanced at the digital clock on the stove. It was after eight. "It's too late now to start anything."

"I was planning on feeding you at my house."

She grinned at him as she smeared mayonnaise on a slice of bread. "What were we going to have?"

"Muffins, strawberry preserves, and chilled champagne." He reached out and swiped a slice of ham. "I was planning on celebrating."

"Yeah, well, about that . . ." She slapped the meat on the bread, and with a vicious blow of the knife cut the sandwich in half.

Owen watched the sharp blade of the knife she was wielding slice through the second sandwich. He swallowed around the knot forming in his throat. "You haven't given me your answer yet." As far as he knew, he had never heard of a man being stabbed for asking a woman to marry him.

She frowned at the sandwiches and dumped a handful of potato chips onto each plate. "Do you have any deep, dark secrets in your past?"

He felt every muscle in his body tighten. "My past is an open book, Nadia. Crow's Head is a very small community. It would be impossible to hide any deep, dark secrets in my closet." He reached out and tenderly stroked the back of her hand with his fingertips. "Does it matter that I don't?"

"No." She turned her hand over and captured his fingers. "But I happen to have a whole closetful." Her lips formed a semismile. "And believe me, it's a real doozie."

"If you share it with me, it will only be half its size."

"It still might be too big for you to handle." Her gaze studied his handsome face. It lovingly caressed his stubborn jaw and seductive lower lip. Her fingers trembled as they clutched his hand harder.

"Why don't you let me be the judge of that?" He squeezed her quivering fingers. "I love you, Nadia, and I will still want you to be my wife, no matter what."

She tried to smile. "Gallant words for a man who doesn't know the facts."

"Give me the facts, love, and let me prove to you they are the truth."

She lowered her gaze to the sandwich in front of her. "Eat your dinner first." She removed her hand from his and nervously played with her pile of potato chips.

Owen grinned and took a huge bite out of his sandwich. The last hurdle to Nadia's heart was about to be breached. She would no longer hide behind her secrets. He had earned her trust. Now all he had to do was earn her love.

Twenty minutes later Owen was in the spare bedroom standing in front of the closet door with a crowbar in his hand. "When you said you had a closetful, you weren't kidding." He jammed the bar in between the door and the jamb and pushed his weight against the crowbar. "Want to tell me again why you nailed the door shut?"

Nadia chewed on her lower lip. "I didn't want anyone accidentally discovering what's behind the door." She grimaced as Owen groaned and attempted to apply more pressure.

"Was there any reason why you had to use so many nails? And why did they have to be *so* big?"

He wrestled the door open another quarter of an inch. "Were you trying to keep people out, or is there something inside that you are trying to keep in?"

Her teeth sank into her lip as the door groaned and finally gave way to his strength. The door popped open and threw Owen off balance. He landed on his butt in front of the closet, clutching the crowbar. There was no turning back now. Her secrets were finally out in the open.

Owen glanced inside the closet. He rubbed a hand over his eyes and looked again. His vision did not change. "Most people have skeletons in their closets, love. But not you." He reached out and lightly fingered the hem of a red sequined gown. "You have clothes in yours." He glanced over his shoulder and up at her. "How original."

"Owen J. Prescott." She reached out and gave him a hand up. "I would like for you to meet my past." She swept her hand toward the packed closet.

Owen glanced between Nadia and the crammed closet. Not receiving any help from Nadia, he took a step closer to the closet and idly shuffled through the hangers. There was enough silk and sequins stuffed into the small closet to keep Elizabeth Taylor happy for a year. Not one gown, lounging outfit, or peignoir set seemed suitable for Nadia. It looked like someone had a relative working in the shipping department of Fredrick's of Hollywood. He glanced at the back of the closet door where a vinyl shoe holder hung. The twenty pockets were jammed with at least thirty-five pairs of spiked heels as tasteless and as gaudy as the clothes. A lone cardboard box sat on the floor buried beneath the long gowns and plastic cleaners' bags protecting most of the clothes. He stroked a cream-colored gown, looked at the tag, and frowned. It was a designer original and pure silk. Nadia had a fortune's worth of clothes nailed shut in a closet. "Do I get an explanation, or am I supposed to guess?"

"It's all in the cardboard box." She reached down and hauled the box out of the closet. "I saved everything I could get my hands on." She picked up the box and handed it to him.

Owen shifted the box and tested its weight. "It's all about you?" he asked in astonishment.

"Not all of it, but I'm one of the key players."

He glanced down at the box and frowned. "Why don't you just tell me about it? That way I can bypass all of this and get the truth at the same time."

"But the public doesn't perceive me in a truthful light, Owen. They only know what they have read or seen on television. For the rest of my life I will be judged by what's in the box."

"So Paul did recognize you from television."

"If he was in New York anytime last summer and there was a television nearby, it would have been impossible for him not to have seen me."

Owen whistled softly. "Now I'm really curious." He tested the box again. "What did you do, commit murder?"

"No, nobody died."

"Am I going to get the truth?"

"After you go through my scrapbooks, and if you're still interested in hearing my side, yes, Owen, I will tell you the truth." She walked to the door. "Why don't you find a comfortable spot to discover what kind of woman you have asked to become your wife? I'll be in the kitchen when you are done."

Owen stood in the silent, empty room clutching the box and listening to her slow footsteps as she went down the stairs. Then he sat down on the carpet, leaned against the wall, opened the box, and confronted Nadia's past.

Nadia poured herself another cup of coffee, took a sip, and dumped the entire cup down the drain. Her stomach couldn't handle another cup of caffeine. Two hours had gone by, and still Owen hadn't left the spare bedroom. And she should have known. She had been sitting in total silence counting the minutes and listening for his footsteps.

She knew what every article in the box said. She had read them all at least a dozen times, most of them more. Every picture was engraved in her memory as if it were yesterday.

Five years ago when she first set foot on American soil, she had one goal set in her mind: to make enough money to bring her family to America. She had arrived with dreams in her head, stars in her eyes, and gold in her heart. America was supposed to be the land of opportunity. A place where dreams came true. After one year of waiting on tables all day and singing in nightclubs all night, she had barely enough money to bring three of her brothers out of Russia. Her family refused her offer—either they were all coming or no one was. She had felt her hopes and dreams slip farther and farther away. Her scrapbook contained a couple of local announcements of her singing, a few publicity photos, but none of her dreams.

The next articles showed her rapid climb to the top. Within months she was singing at one of the top nightclubs in Manhattan and receiving an astronomical salary. She was also linked to one of New York's most notorious mobsters, Anthony Ciotti, better known as Big C. She shared a luxury apartment overlooking Central Park with him and acted as his hostess on numerous occasions. The FBI was trying to build a case against Big C for racketeering, but they could never get enough evidence. The climax came when the IRS finally nailed him on income-tax evasion. The trial made front-page news every evening, and she was labeled the Manhattan Mistress who wouldn't talk. Big C got five to seven in the state pen, and the Manhattan Mistress dropped out of sight.

Nadia paced over to the screen door and stared off into the night. There was nothing in that box to explain her actions. Owen would have no reason to doubt those articles. For all appearances she had been Anthony Ciotti's lover and confidante.

She sighed and leaned her cheek against the cool metal of the screen door. Two hungry mosquitoes, sensing a warm victim, buzzed against the screen. It would have been easier to have told Owen the truth first and then let him see the articles, but she had to know. Did he trust her enough to realize she could never be that woman in those articles? Did he love her enough to want to know the truth? A third mosquito joined the first two.

The creaking of the ceiling joists told her the wait was over. Owen was heading for the stairs.

TWELVE

Owen entered the kitchen and glanced at the back of the woman staring out into the night. Then, placing a couple of photos on the kitchen table, he headed for the coffeepot. He could go for something stronger, such as a bottle of Wyatt Marshall's twenty-year-old Scotch, but he settled for a cup of Nadia's coffee instead. He leaned against the counter and softly said, "That was some of the best fiction I've ever read."

Nadia slowly turned around. "Fiction?"

"You didn't honestly think that I would believe any of that."

"The part about Big C going to jail for income-tax evasion is true." She moved away from the door and glanced at the photos lying on the kitchen table. They were all photos of her.

"The man was guilty of a lot more than that." He watched as she shuffled through the pictures.

She shrugged her shoulders. "Probably." She picked up a black-and-white photo of herself taken four years ago when she'd first arrived in America. She looked so young and naive, full of hopes and dreams. "Tony had one sterling quality; he loved his wife and children."

"Wife? There was no mention of any wife or children."

She dropped the picture back onto the pile. "I know." She glanced at Owen. "How come you don't believe what's written in black-and-white?"

He placed the cup on the table. "I know you, Nadia. You could no more be some mobster's plaything than I could be a rock-and-roll star."

Nadia looked at him deadpan. "I've heard you sing in the shower, Owen."

He reached out and tenderly cupped her cheek. "Then you know I can't carry a tune. You'd better hope our children get their singing from you and their patience from me." He brushed her lips with a soft kiss.

"Children?" whispered Nadia. "Then you still want to marry me without even knowing the truth?"

"How could you doubt it?" He covered her mouth with a deep, hungry kiss that would leave her without any doubts about his desire. He ended the kiss and pulled back slightly. "I have to admit that I'm mighty curious as to why you were living with a married man, and a famed mobster to boot."

"Two boots?"

Owen chuckled and sat on one of the kitchen chairs, pulling her down onto his lap. "Forget the boots, it's only a saying. You have five minutes to explain about Big C."

She wrapped her arms around his neck and wiggled. "Why only five minutes?"

He held her still. "Because that's about how long I can hold out without making love to you."

She grinned for a moment before reaching for a picture and turning serious. "This is me four years ago when I was right off the boat. I'd just landed my first singing job at some little piano bar."

"I can tell."

"How?" She glanced at the photo. She had been wearing the same red dress she had worn to dinner with Owen on their first date.

"The eyes." He spread out the pictures and lined them up in perfect chronological order. "See"—he pointed to the first photo—"here you are happy, and your eyes are filled with dreams." His finger moved to the next photo. "This one you are still dreaming, but it's becoming harder."

"That's when I realized it was going to take more than hard work and dreams to get my family out of war-torn Europe."

"In this one the dreaming had stopped." His finger moved on. "And then here is where the secrets began."

Nadia bit her lip and studied the publicity photo. "One night after I was done with my set, a very wealthy gentleman paid me a visit. He offered me a deal I couldn't refuse." She stood up and walked away from the table and Owen. "It seemed this gentleman had a grown daughter, Maria, whom he loved very much, and he was willing to go to any lengths to protect her. Maria fell in love with a man whom she knew her father would never approve of and was secretly married."

"Anthony Ciotti," muttered Owen.

"How you say, binko?"

"It's 'bingo,' love. Continue."

"Tony and Maria kept their marriage a secret from everyone until the first baby was on its way. They told Maria's father, and as you can imagine, all hell broke lose. Tony hid Maria and their young son and tried to make a name for himself the only way he knew how, on the streets. As his reputation and wealth grew, so did his list of enemies. Maria and her father talked and fought constantly. She refused to leave Tony and was now carrying their second child. Maria's father realized that Maria and his grandchildren needed more protection than Tony could provide. No one, not even Tony's closest associates, knew of his family. Tony's enemies were starting to dig around, trying to find his weak spot."

"So Maria's father hired you to play Tony's mistress," guessed Owen.

"I wouldn't take any money from Tony, because I wasn't exactly sure where it was coming from, but Maria's father was another story. His money came from shipping lines and fiber optics, and all of it was legit. Between his money and the money I was then making at the nightclub, I saved enough to bring my entire family over."

"Didn't Maria mind that you were living with Tony?"

"I didn't live with Tony, Owen." She paced the kitchen floor. "We were all play-acting. Maria's father set her and the children up in a fancy apartment in Manhattan. Tony and I had the apartment next door. There were three apartments on our floor, Maria's, mine, and some jet-setting playboy who was never in New York. Tony would pick me up at the club, and we'd go home together every night. He went to Maria's apartment, and I went to mine. A couple of times we held a party in my apartment as a front. For two years we played our parts and fooled the world and his enemies." She smiled at some distant memory. "I even baby-sat a couple times so that Maria and he could spend some time alone."

Owen glanced down at the last couple of photos and now understood the secrets filling her eyes. For two years his Nadia had ceased to exist. No wonder he had a hard time relating these pictures to the woman he loved. They were two entirely different people. She had sacrificed twenty-four months of her life for the love of her family. "Was it worth it?"

She glanced at the glamorous, if not sometimes gaudy, woman staring up at her from the photos and softly smiled. Her past was lying out in front of the man she loved, and he hadn't run in terror or disgust.

"I'd do it again if I had to." She glanced around the kitchen. "Some good did come out of it. I didn't have to wait on tables all day, so I worked on my children's songs. By the time the trial ended, I had enough to contact a record company that had shown interest in my idea for a children's album."

"What happened to Tony and Maria?"

"After he was sentenced, she gave him a choice: either accept her father's offer of a job in a foreign country when he was released from prison or she wouldn't be there when they unlocked the gates. It seems Maria had got tired of seeing her husband's picture plastered all over the newspaper with me on his arm, and she said the boys needed a father." Nadia stacked the pictures into one neat pile. "Last I heard, Tony will be moving to Brazil in a couple of years."

Owen drummed his fingers on the table. "Do you ever hear from any of them?"

"Nope. Maria's father knows where I live, though. Two days after I moved here, IRS arrived with a note of thanks from him. He was eternally grateful that I never spilled the beans about Tony having a wife and all during the trial."

"You lied on the stand?" His fingers stilled.

"Of course not. This is America. I could go to jail for lying in court. No one even asked me if Tony had a wife. They kept questioning me about his business, and I told them the truth. I knew nothing."

Owen stood up. "So now I know all your secrets." He slowly advanced toward her.

"I would appreciate it if you don't go spilling the beans to my family about how I saved enough to bring them all over."

"How do they think you made that much money?"

"This is America, Owen. They still believe that anything is possible."

"Really?" He backed her against the counter and placed a hand on either side of her. His pleasant expression vanished. "If you ever pull another stunt like that again, I will personally take you over my knee and spank you so that you won't be able to sit for a week."

Nadia's eyes opened wider, and she pressed her back into the Formica countertop. "What are you yelling for?"

"Because I'm furious with you." He smacked his sore hand against the counter and grimaced as pain shot up his arm. "Don't you have any idea what could have happened to you?" he demanded.

"I . . ."

"Surely you aren't that naive not to know what kind of danger you were exposed to." He crowded her against the counter and shouted, "Don't they have thugs in Russia?" He didn't know if he wanted to harangue her or kiss her senseless. He raised his hand and tenderly brushed her cheek. "You could have been killed."

She watched in wonder as his gaze caressed her face. "I wasn't." She reached up and traced the frown pulling at the corner of his mouth. "When things got a little risky, Tony hired a bodyguard for me."

Owen pushed away from the counter and thrust his fingers through his hair. "Lord, Nadia, didn't you see the danger?"

"Every day." Her gaze followed him as he paced in front of her. "I also saw the danger of having my family stay in an unstabilized country. I saw the killing and the fighting every day on CNN, and I prayed I wouldn't see anyone I knew lying dead in the streets from sniper fire or another senseless round of mortars."

Owen froze and really looked at Nadia. The fear she had been feeling still had the power to shake her voice. What would he have done if it had been his family over there? Would he have had the courage to risk his own life to bring them to safety? He liked to think he would have, but Nadia had proved she did possess such courage. He opened his arms and said, "I didn't think it was possible, but I think I love you more."

She flew into his arms murmuring some melodic Russian words.

He laughed and hugged her tighter. "That sounds familiar—what does it mean?' He remembered she had whispered those same words deep into the night.

"It's Russian for 'I love you.' " She smiled radiantly and reached for his mouth.

Owen swept her up into his arms and headed for the stairs. "Your five minutes are up."

She ran her hand down his chest and over the front of his jeans. She chuckled when he nearly lost his balance on the first step. "That's not all that's up."

He shifted her weight and continued up the steps, grinning. "Have you no shame, woman!"

Nadia threw back her head and laughed with pure joy. "No, Owen, the shame is gone along with the secrets. With you I have only love and honor."

He slowly lowered her to her feet beside the bed. He reached over and turned on the light. His gaze bore into hers. This was the Nadia who first came to America. Her eyes glistened with hopes and dreams for the future. There wasn't even the faintest shadow of the secrets she had carried so bravely. "Lord, how I love you." He pulled her into his arms and kissed her with the promise of fulfilling every one of her dreams.

Nadia smiled against his warm chest. In his sleep his breathing was slow and even. She reached down to pull up the sheet as a cool evening breeze stirred the curtains. After a moment she gave up and wrote it off as a lost cause. The sheet was helplessly tangled beneath Owen's legs, and she hadn't the heart to wake him. She slowly reached over the side of the bed and pulled up the quilt that had been pushed to the floor during their lovemaking.

She gently tucked the quilt around their naked bodies and snuggled back into his arms. Even in sleep his arms cradled her so tenderly. She laid her head back down onto his chest and closed her eyes and welcomed sleep.

A moment later her eyes flew open, but she didn't move a muscle. She didn't even breathe. There it was! She hadn't imagined it. A soft melody teased the corner of her mind and grew with each passing moment. It was a song full of hopes, dreams, and love. It was a song about a wise old owl named Owen who refused to give up. Nadia closed her eyes and allowed the music to wash over her, to surround her with its simple joy. How fitting it was that she was composing the last song for the album as she lay in Owen's loving arms.

EPILOGUE

"Nadia, if we don't hurry, we are going to miss the plane," said Owen. He traded Sebastian his three-year-old son, Jeremiah, for the two suitcases the butler had just carried down the stairs.

"I'm coming!" shouted Nadia from the kitchen, where she was giving Milly and her mother last-minute instructions on eighteen-month-old Zachary's schedule. "Now, remember, he doesn't like green vegetables, only yellow ones." She double-checked to make sure their itinerary was taped to the front of the refrigerator, complete with hotels, phone numbers, and emergency numbers. "Make sure he drinks his milk, and don't let him eat the soap in the bathtub again."

"You are only going for ten days, Nadia," pleaded her mother. "I think I can handle my own grandchild for ten days." She scooped the grinning Zachary from his high chair and whispered loving words to the child in Russian.

"Nadia!" cried Owen from the foyer. "Did you remember to pack your vitamin pills?"

She reached on top of the refrigerator, grabbed the huge blue bottle of prenatal vitamin pills, and dropped them into her purse. "Yes, dear." She gave her slightly rounded tummy a gentle pat and followed her mother, Milly, and her son out of the kitchen. "Did you remember the tickets?"

Owen checked his pocket. "Yes." He spotted his wife as she took Zachary from his grandmother's arms. "The driver is waiting outside, love."

Nadia gave her son a kiss and a big hug. "Let him wait a moment longer." She gave him another noisy kiss before handing him over to Owen. She reached for little Jeremiah sitting on Sebastian's shoulder. "Come here, lovely, and give your mommy another kiss." Jeremiah came willingly. "Now, you promise to be a good boy for Aunt Verna, and Grandmom and Papa, and for Sebastian and Milly, and for Uncle Stevo and Aunt Yelena . . ."

"Sweetheart, if you name all your family staying here to take care of two little boys, we will surely miss the plane, and how will that look? Your first European tour, and you'll miss your debut." He took Jeremiah from his wife's arms and handed him to Milosh.

Nadia gazed at the angelic faces of her sons and felt the tears start to burn in the back of her eyes. "Maybe we should wait until—"

Owen pulled her out of the door as Sebastian hurried in front of them with the luggage. "You promised the record company and your little fans an eight-city tour two years ago."

"That was before I knew I was pregnant with Zachary." She glanced over her shoulder and waved to everyone crowding out the front door to wish them farewell.

"If we don't go now, it will be another two years." He glanced at her stomach and grinned. "Winslow will need his mommy home with him for the first couple of months."

"I'm not naming our baby Winslow." She protectively laid her hand against the slight bulge as Owen helped her into the backseat. "Who's to say it isn't a girl, anyhow?"

Owen waved to his sons and their twelve baby-sitters as the limo pulled away from the house. He glanced at his wife and grinned. "Sofia swiped your teacup the other day and read the leaves." He reached over and kissed her motherly concern away. Their sons were in great hands, and he was finally going to have Nadia all to himself. Just him and a couple of thousand adoring little fans. "She said she saw blue again." He glanced at the smoked privacy glass separating them from the driver and grinned. Pulling her into his arms, he whispered, "Lots and lots of blue." His mouth slanted down onto hers, and neither one of them paid any attention to the miles that rolled away as they headed for the airport.

THE EDITOR'S CORNER

The coming month brings to mind lions and lambs—
not only because of the weather but also because of our
six wonderful LOVESWEPTs. In these books you'll find
fierce and feisty, warm and gentle characters who add
up to a rich and exciting array of people whose stories
of falling in love are enthralling.

Judy Gill starts things off this month with another
terrific story in **KISS AND MAKE UP,** LOVESWEPT
#678. He'd never been around when they were mar-
ried, but now that Kat Waddell has decided to hire
a nanny to help with the kids, her ex-husband, Rand,
insists he's perfect for the job! Accepting his offer means
letting him live in the basement apartment—too dangerously close for a man whose presence arouses potent
memories of reckless passion . . . and painful images of
love gone wrong. He married Kat hoping for the perfect fantasy family, but the pretty picture he'd imagined
didn't include an unhappy wife he never seemed to sat-

isfy . . . except in bed. Now Rand needs to show Kat he's changed. The sensual magic he weaves makes her feel cherished at last, but Kat wonders if it's enough to mend their broken vows. Judy's special touch makes this story of love reborn especially poignant.

It's on to Scotland for **LORD OF THE ISLAND**, LOVESWEPT #679, by the wonderfully talented Kimberli Wagner. Ian MacLeod is annoyed by the American woman who comes to stay on Skye during the difficult winter months, but when Tess Hartley sheds her raingear, the laird is enchanted by the dark-eyed siren whose fiery temper reveals a rebel who won't be ordered around by any man—even him! He expects pity, even revulsion at the evidence of his terrible accident, but Tess's pain runs as deep as his does, and her artist's eye responds to Ian's scarred face with wonder at his courage . . . and a wildfire hunger to lose herself in his arms. As always, Kimberli weaves an intense story of love and triumph you won't soon forget.

Victoria Leigh gives us a hero who is rough, rugged, and capable of **DANGEROUS LOVE**, LOVESWEPT #680. Four years earlier, he'd fallen in love with her picture, but when Luke Sinclair arrives on her secluded island to protect his boss's sister from the man who'd once kidnapped her, he is stunned to find that Elisabeth Connor is more exquisite than he'd dreamed—and not nearly as fragile as he'd feared. Instead, she warms to the fierce heat of his gaze, begging to know the ecstacy of his touch. Even though he's sworn to protect her with his life, Elisabeth must make him see that she wants him to share it with her instead. Only Victoria could deliver a romance that's as sexy and fun as it is touching.

We're delighted to have another fabulous book from Laura Taylor this month, and **WINTER HEART**, LOVESWEPT #681, is Laura at her best. Suspicious that the elegant blonde has a hidden agenda when she hires him to restore a family mansion, Jack McMillan quickly puts Mariah Chandler on the defensive—and is shocked to feel a flash flood of heat and desire rush through him! He believes she is only a spoiled rich girl indulging a whim, but he can't deny the hunger that ignites within him to possess her. Tantalized by sensual longings she's never expected to feel, Mariah surrenders to the dizzying pleasure of Jack's embrace. She's fought her demons by helping other women who have suffered but has never told Jack of the shadows that still haunt her nights. Now Mariah must heal his wounded spirit by finally sharing her pain and daring him to share a future.

Debra Dixon brings together a hot, take-charge Cajun and a sizzling TV seductress in **MIDNIGHT HOUR,** LOVESWEPT #682. Her voice grabs his soul and turns him inside out before he even sees her, but when Dr. Nick Devereaux gazes at Midnight Mercy Malone, the town's TV horror-movie hostess, he aches to muss her gorgeous russet hair . . . and make love to the lady until she moans his name! Still, he likes her even better out of her slinky costumes, an everyday enchantress who tempts him to make regular house calls. His sexy accent gives her goosebumps, but Mercy hopes her lusty alter ego might scare off a man she fears will choose work over her. Yet, his kisses send her up in flames and make her ache for love that never ends. Debra's spectacular romance will leave you breathless.

Olivia Rupprecht invites you to a **SHOTGUN WEDDING,** LOVESWEPT #683. Aaron Breedlove once fled his mountain hamlet to escape his desire for Addy McDonald, but now fate has brought him back—and his father's deathbed plea has given him no choice but to keep the peace between the clans and marry his dangerous obsession! With hair as dark as a moonlit night, Addy smells of wildflowers and rainwater, and Aaron can deny his anguished passion no longer. He is the knight in shining armor she's always dreamed of, but Addy yearns to become his wife in every way—and

Aaron refuses to accept her gift or surrender his soul. **SHOTGUN WEDDING** is a sensual, steamy romance that Olivia does like no one else.

Happy reading,

With warmest wishes,

Nita Taublib

Nita Taublib

Associate Publisher

P.S. Don't miss the spectacular women's novels coming from Bantam in April: **DARK PARADISE** is the dangerously erotic novel of romantic suspense from nationally bestselling author Tami Hoag; **WARRIOR BRIDE** is a sizzling medieval romance in the bestselling tradition of Julie Garwood from Tamara Leigh, a dazzling new author; **REBEL IN SILK** is the fabulous new *Once Upon a Time* romance from bestselling Loveswept author Sandra Chastain. We'll be giving you a sneak peek at these terrific books in next month's LOVESWEPTs. And immediately following this page, look for a preview of the spectacular women's fiction books from Bantam *available now*!

Don't miss these exciting books by your favorite Bantam authors

On sale in February:

SILK AND STONE
by Deborah Smith

LADY DANGEROUS
by Suzanne Robinson

SINS OF INNOCENCE
by Jean Stone

Deborah Smith

SILK AND STONE

She had everything ready for him, everything but herself. What could she say to a husband she hadn't seen or spoken to in ten years: *Hi, honey, how'd your decade go?*

The humor was nervous, and morbid. She knew that. Samantha Raincrow hurt for him, hurt in ways she couldn't put into words. Ten years of waiting, of thinking about what he was going through, of *why* he'd been subjected to it, had worn her down to bare steel.

What he'd endured would always be her fault.

She moved restlessly around the finest hotel suite in the city, obsessed with straightening fresh flowers that were already perfectly arranged in their vases. He wouldn't have seen many flowers. She wanted him to remember the scent of youth and freedom. Of love.

Broad windows looked out over Raleigh. A nice city for a reunion. The North Carolina summer had just begun; the trees still wore the dark shades of new spring leaves.

She wanted everything to be new for him, but knew it could never be, that they were both haunted by the past—betrayals that couldn't be undone. She was Alexandra Lomax's niece; she couldn't scrub that stain out of her blood.

Her gifts were arranged around the suite's sitting room; Sam went to them and ran her hands over each one. A silk tapestry, six-feet-square and woven in geometrics from an old Cherokee design, was draped over a chair. She wanted him to see one of the ways she'd spent all the hours alone. Lined up in a precise row along one wall were five large boxes filled with letters she'd written to him and never sent, because he wouldn't have read them. A journal of every day. On a desk in front of the windows were stacks of bulging photo albums. One was filled with snapshots of her small apartment in California, the car she'd bought second-hand, years ago, and still drove, more of her tapestries, and her loom. And the Cove. Pictures of the wild Cove, and the big log house where he'd been born. She wanted him to see how lovingly she'd cared for it over the years.

The other albums were filled with her modeling portfolio. A strange one, by most standards. Just hands. Her hands, the only beautiful thing about her, holding soaps and perfumes and jewelry, caressing lingerie and detergent and denture cleaner, and a thousand other products. Because she wanted him to understand everything about her work, she'd brought the DeMeda book, too—page after over-sized, sensual page of black-and-white art photos. Photos of her fingertips touching a man's glistening, naked back, or molded to the crest of a muscular, bare thigh.

If he cared, she would explain about the ludicrous amount of money she'd gotten for that work, and that the book had been created by a famous photographer, and was considered an art form. If he cared, she'd assure him that there was nothing provocative about standing under hot studio lights with her hands cramping, while beautiful, half-clothed male models yawned and told her about their latest boyfriends.

If he cared.

Last, she went to a small, rectangular folder on a coffee table near the room's sofa. She sat down and opened it, her hands shaking so badly she could barely grasp the folder. The new deed for the Cove, with both his name and hers on it, was neatly tucked inside. She'd promised to transfer title to him the day he came home. If she hadn't held her ownership of the Cove over him like a threat all these years, he would have divorced her.

She hadn't promised to let him have it without her.

Sam hated that coercion, and knew he hated it, too. It was too much like something her Aunt Alexandra would have done. But Sam would not lose him, not without fighting for a second chance.

The phone rang. She jumped up, scattering the paperwork on the carpet, and ran to answer. "Dreyfus delivery service," said a smooth, elegantly drawling voice. "I have one slightly-used husband for you, ma'am."

Their lawyer's black sense of humor didn't help matters. Her heart pounded, and she felt dizzy. "Ben, you're downstairs?"

"Yes, in the lobby. Actually, I'm in the lobby. He's in the men's room, changing clothes."

"Changing clothes?"

"He asked me to stop on the way here. I perform many functions, Sam, but helping my clients pick a new outfit is a first."

"Why in the world—"

"He didn't want you to see him in what they gave him to wear. In a manner of speaking, he wanted to look like a civilian, again."

Sam inhaled raggedly and bowed her head, pressing her fingertips under her eyes, pushing hard. She wouldn't cry, wouldn't let him see her for the first time in ten years with her face swollen and her nose running. Small dignities were all she had left. "Has he said anything?" she asked, when she could trust herself to speak calmly.

"Hmmm, lawyer-client confidentiality, Sam. I represent both of you. What kind of lawyer do you think I am? Never mind, I don't want to hear the brutal truth."

"One who's become a good friend."

Ben hesitated. "Idle flattery." Then, slowly, "He said he would walk away without ever seeing you, again, if he could."

She gripped the phone numbly. *That's no worse than you expected*, she told herself. But she felt dead inside. "Tell him the doors to the suite will be open."

"All right. I'm sure he needs all the open doors he can get."

"I can't leave them all open. If I did, I'd lose him." Ben didn't ask what she meant; he'd helped her engineer some of those closed doors.

"Parole is not freedom," Ben said. "He understands that."

"And I'm sure he's thrilled that he's being forced to live with a wife he doesn't want."

"I suspect he doesn't know what he wants, at the moment."

"He's always known, Ben. That's the problem."

She said good-bye, put the phone down and walked with leaden resolve to the suite's double doors. She opened them and stepped back. For a moment, she considered checking herself in a mirror one last time, turned halfway, then realized she was operating on the assumption that what she looked like mattered to him. So she faced the doors and waited.

Each faint whir and rumble of the elevators down the hall made her nerves dance. She could barely breathe, listening for the sound of those doors opening. She smoothed her upswept hair, then anxiously fingered a blond strand that had escaped. Jerking at each hair, she pulled them out. A dozen or more, each unwilling to go. If it hurt, she didn't notice.

She clasped her hands in front of her pale yellow suitdress, then unclasped them, fiddled with the gold braid along the neck, twisted the plain gold wedding band on her left hand. She never completely removed it from her body, even when she worked. It had either remained on her finger or on a sturdy gold chain around her neck, all these years.

That chain, lying coldly between her breasts, also held his wedding ring.

She heard the hydraulic purr of an elevator settling into place, then the softer rush of metal doors sliding apart. Ten years compressed in the nerve-wracking space of a few seconds. If he weren't the one walking up the long hall right now, if some unsuspecting stranger strolled by instead, she thought her shaking legs would collapse.

Damn the thick carpeting. She couldn't gauge his steps. She wasn't ready. No, she would always be ready. Her life stopped, and she was waiting, waiting . . .

He walked into the doorway and halted. This tall, broad-shouldered stranger was her husband. Every memory she had of his appearance was there, stamped with a brutal decade of maturity, but there. Except for the look in his eyes. Nothing had ever been bleak and hard about him before. He stared at her with an intensity that could have burned her shadow on the floor.

Words were hopeless, but all that they had. "Welcome back," she said. Then, brokenly, "*Jake*."

He took a deep breath, as if a shiver had run through him. He closed the doors without ever taking his eyes off her. Then he was at her in two long steps, grasping her by the shoulders, lifting her to her toes. They were close enough to share a breath, a heartbeat. "I trained myself not to think about you," he said, his voice a raw whisper. "Because if I had, I would have lost my mind."

"I never deserted you. I wanted to be part of your life, but you wouldn't let me. Will you please try now?"

"Do you still have it?" he asked.

Anger. Defeat. The hoarse sound she made contained both. "Yes."

He released her. "Good. That's all that matters."

Sam turned away, tears coming helplessly. After all these years, there was still only one thing he wanted from her, and it was the one thing she hated, a symbol of pride and obsession she would never understand, a blood-red stone that had controlled the lives of too many people already, including theirs.

The Pandora ruby.

LADY DANGEROUS
by
Suzanne Robinson

"An author with star quality . . . spectacularly talented."
—Romantic Times

Liza Elliot had a very good reason for posing as a maid in the house of the notorious Viscount Radcliffe. It was the only way the daring beauty could discover whether this sinister nobleman had been responsible for her brother's murder. But Liza never knew how much she risked until the night she came face-to-face with the dangerously arresting and savagely handsome viscount himself . . .

Iron squealed against iron as the footmen swung the gates back again. Black horses trotted into view, two pairs, drawing a black lacquered carriage. Liza stirred uneasily as she realized that vehicle, tack, and coachman were all in unrelieved black. Polished brass lanterns and fittings provided the only contrast.

The carriage pulled up before the house, the horses stamping and snorting in the cold. The coachman, wrapped in a driving coat and muffled in a black scarf, made no sound as he controlled the ill-tempered menace of his animals. She couldn't help leaning forward a bit, in spite of her growing trepidation. Perhaps it was the eeriness of the fog-drenched night, or the unnerving appearance of the shining black and silent carriage, but no one moved.

Then she saw it. A boot. A black boot unlike any she'd ever seen. High of heel, tapered in the toe, scuffed, and sticking out of the carriage window. Its owner must be reclining inside. As she closed her mouth, which had fallen open, Liza saw a puff of smoke billow out from the interior. So aghast was she at this unorthodox arrival, she didn't hear the duke and his brother come down the steps to stand near her.

Suddenly the boot was withdrawn. The head footman immediately jumped forward and opened the carriage door. The interior lamps hadn't been lit. From the darkness stepped a man so tall, he had to curl almost double to keep his hat from hitting the roof of the vehicle.

The footman retreated as the man straightened. Liza sucked in her breath, and a feeling of unreality swamped her other emotions. The man who stood before her wore clothing so dark, he seemed a part of the night and the gloom of the carriage that had borne him. A low-crowned hat with a wide brim concealed his face, and he wore a long coat that flared away from his body. It was open, and he brushed one edge of it back where it revealed buckskin pants, a vest, a black, low-slung belt and holster bearing a gleaming revolver.

He paused, undisturbed by the shock he'd created. Liza suddenly remembered a pamphlet she'd seen on the American West. That's where she'd seen a man like this. Not anywhere in England, but in illustrations of the American badlands.

At last the man moved. He struck a match on his belt and lit a thin cigar. The tip glowed, and for a moment his face was revealed in the light of the match. She glimpsed black, black hair, so dark it seemed to absorb the flame of the match. Thick lashes lifted to reveal the glitter of cat-green eyes, a straight nose, and a chin that bore a day's stubble. The match died and was tossed aside. The man hooked his thumbs in his belt and sauntered down the line of servants, ignoring them.

He stopped in front of the duke, puffed on the cigar, and stared at the older man. Slowly, a pretense of a smile spread over his face. He removed the cigar from his mouth, shoved his hat back on his head, and spoke for the first time.

"Well, well, well. Evening, Daddy."

That accent, it was so strange—a hot, heavy drawl spiked with cool and nasty amusement. This man took his time with words, caressed them, savored them, and made his enemies wait in apprehension for him to complete them. The duke bristled, and his white hair almost stood out like a lion's mane as he gazed at his son.

"Jocelin, you forget yourself."

The cigar sailed to the ground and hissed as it hit the damp pavement. Liza longed to shrink back from the sudden viciousness that sprang from the viscount's eyes. The viscount smiled again and spoke softly, with relish and an evil amusement. The drawl vanished, to be supplanted by a clipped, aristocratic accent.

"I don't forget. I'll never forget. Forgetting is your vocation, one you've elevated to a sin, or you wouldn't bring my dear uncle where I could get my hands on him."

All gazes fastened on the man standing behind the duke. Though much younger than his brother, Yale Marshall had the same thick hair, black as his brother's had once been, only gray at the temples. Of high stature like his nephew, he reminded Liza of the illustrations of knights in *La Morte d'Arthur*, for he personified doomed beauty and chivalry. He had the same startling green eyes as his nephew, and he gazed at the viscount sadly as the younger man faced him.

Yale murmured to his brother, "I told you I shouldn't have come."

With knightly dignity he stepped aside, and the movement brought him nearer to his nephew. Jocelin's left hand touched the revolver on his hip as his uncle turned. The duke hissed his name, and the hand dropped loosely to his side. He lit another cigar.

At a glance from his face, the butler suddenly sprang into motion. He ran up the steps to open the door. The duke marched after him, leaving his son to follow, slowly, after taking a few leisurely puffs on his cigar.

"Ah, well," he murmured. "I can always kill him later."

SINS OF INNOCENCE
by
JEAN STONE

They were four women with only one thing in common: each gave up her baby to a stranger. They'd met in a home for unwed mothers, where all they had to hold on to was each other. Now, twenty-five years later, it's time to go back and face the past. The date is set for a reunion with the children they have never known. But who will find the courage to attend?

"I've decided to find my baby," Jess said.

Susan picked up a spoon and stirred in a hefty teaspoon of sugar from the bowl. She didn't usually take sugar, but she needed to keep her hands busy. Besides, if she tried to drink from the mug now, she'd probably drop it.

"What's that got to do with me?"

Jess took a sip, then quickly put down the mug. It's probably still too hot, Susan thought. She probably burned the Estée Lauder right off her lips.

"I . . ." The woman stammered, not looking Susan in the eye, "I was wondering if you've ever had the same feelings."

The knot that had found its way into Susan's stomach increased in size.

"I have a son," Susan said.

Jess looked into her mug. "So do I. In fact, I have two sons and a daughter. And"—she picked up the mug to try again—"a husband."

Susan pushed back her hair. *My* baby, she thought. *David's baby.* She closed her eyes, trying to envision what he would look like today. He'd be a man. Older even than David had been when . . .

How could she tell Jess that 1968 had been the biggest regret of her life? How could she tell this woman she no longer knew that she felt the decisions she'd made then had led her in a direction that had no definition, no purpose? But years ago Susan had accepted one important thing: She couldn't go back.

"So why do you want to do this?"

Jess looked across the table at Susan. "Because it's time," she said.

Susan hesitated before asking the next question. "What do you want from me?"

Jess set down her mug and began twisting the ring again. "Haven't you ever wondered? About your baby?"

Only a million times. Only every night when I go to bed. Only every day as I've watched Mark grow and blossom. Only every time I see a boy who is the same age.

"What are you suggesting?"

"I'm planning a reunion. With our children. I've seen Miss Taylor, and she's agreed to help. She knows where they all are."

"*All* of them?"

"Yours. Mine. P.J.'s and Ginny's. I'm going to

contact everyone, even the kids. Whoever shows up, shows up. Whoever doesn't, doesn't. It's a chance we'll all be taking, but we'll be doing it together. *Together*. The way we got through it in the first place."

The words hit Susan like a rapid fire of a BB gun at a carnival. She stood and walked across the room. She straightened the stack of laundry. "I think you're out of your mind," she said.

And don't miss these heart-stopping
romances from Bantam Books,
on sale in March:

DARK PARADISE
by the nationally bestselling author
Tami Hoag
"Tami Hoag belongs at the top of
everyone's favorite author list"
—*Romantic Times*

WARRIOR BRIDE
by Tamara Leigh
"... a passionate love story that captures all
the splendor of the medieval era."
—nationally bestselling author
Teresa Medeiros

REBEL IN SILK
by Sandra Chastain
"Sandra Chastain's characters' steamy
relationships are the stuff dreams are
made of."
—*Romantic Times*

OFFICIAL RULES

To enter the sweepstakes below carefully follow all instructions found elsewhere in this offer.

The **Winners Classic** will award prizes with the following approximate maximum values: 1 Grand Prize: $26,500 (or $25,000 cash alternate); 1 First Prize: $3,000; 5 Second Prizes: $400 each; 35 Third Prizes: $100 each; 1,000 Fourth Prizes: $7.50 each. Total maximum retail value of Winners Classic Sweepstakes is $42,500. Some presentations of this sweepstakes may contain individual entry numbers corresponding to one or more of the aforementioned prize levels. To determine the Winners, individual entry numbers will first be compared with the winning numbers preselected by computer. For winning numbers not returned, prizes will be awarded in random drawings from among all eligible entries received. Prize choices may be offered at various levels. If a winner chooses an automobile prize, all license and registration fees, taxes, destination charges and, other expenses not offered herein are the responsibility of the winner. If a winner chooses a trip, travel must be complete within one year from the time the prize is awarded. Minors must be accompanied by an adult. Travel companion(s) must also sign release of liability. Trips are subject to space and departure availability. Certain black-out dates may apply.

The following applies to the sweepstakes named above:

No purchase necessary. You can also enter the sweepstakes by sending your name and address to: P.O. Box 508, Gibbstown, N.J. 08027. Mail each entry separately. Sweepstakes begins 6/1/93. Entries must be received by 12/30/94. Not responsible for lost, late, damaged, misdirected, illegible or postage due mail. Mechanically reproduced entries are not eligible. All entries become property of the sponsor and will not be returned.

Prize Selection/Validations: Selection of winners will be conducted no later than 5:00 PM on January 28, 1995, by an independent judging organization whose decisions are final. Random drawings will be held at 1211 Avenue of the Americas, New York, N.Y. 10036. Entrants need not be present to win. Odds of winning are determined by total number of entries received. Circulation of this sweepstakes is estimated not to exceed 200 million. All prizes are guaranteed to be awarded and delivered to winners. Winners will be notified by mail and may be required to complete an affidavit of eligibility and release of liability which must be returned within 14 days of date on notification or alternate winners will be selected in a random drawing. Any prize notification letter or any prize returned to a participating sponsor, Bantam Doubleday Dell Publishing Group, Inc., its participating divisions or subsidiaries, or the independent judging organization as undeliverable will be awarded to an alternate winner. Prizes are not transferable. No substitution for prizes except as offered or as may be necessary due to unavailability, in which case a prize of equal or greater value will be awarded. Prizes will be awarded approximately 90 days after the drawing. All taxes are the sole responsibility of the winners. Entry constitutes permission (except where prohibited by law) to use winners' names, hometowns, and likenesses for publicity purposes without further or other compensation. Prizes won by minors will be awarded in the name of parent or legal guardian.

Participation: Sweepstakes open to residents of the United States and Canada, except for the province of Quebec. Sweepstakes sponsored by Bantam Doubleday Dell Publishing Group, Inc., (BDD), 1540 Broadway, New York, NY 10036. Versions of this sweepstakes with different graphics and prize choices will be offered in conjunction with various solicitations or promotions by different subsidiaries and divisions of BDD. Where applicable, winners will have their choice of any prize offered at level won. Employees of BDD, its divisions, subsidiaries, advertising agencies, independent judging organization, and their immediate family members are not eligible.

Canadian residents, in order to win, must first correctly answer a time limited arithmetical skill testing question. Void in Puerto Rico, Quebec and wherever prohibited or restricted by law. Subject to all federal, state, local and provincial laws and regulations. For a list of major prize winners (available after 1/29/95): send a self-addressed, stamped envelope entirely separate from your entry to: Sweepstakes Winners, P.O. Box 517, Gibbstown, NJ 08027. Requests must be received by 12/30/94. DO NOT SEND ANY OTHER CORRESPONDENCE TO THIS P.O. BOX.

Don't miss these fabulous Bantam women's fiction titles

Now on Sale

● SILK AND STONE by Deborah Smith

From MIRACLE to BLUE WILLOW, Deborah Smith's evocative novels won a special place in reader's hearts. Now, from the author hailed by critics as "a uniquely significant voice in contemporary women's fiction," comes a spellbinding, unforgettably romantic new work. Vibrant with wit, aching with universal emotion, SILK AND STONE is Deborah Smith at her most triumphant.

_____29689-2 $5.99/$6.99 in Canada

● LADY DANGEROUS
by Suzanne Robinson

Liza Elliot had a very good reason for posing as a maid in the house of the notorious Viscount Radcliffe. It was the only way the daring beauty could discover whether this sinister nobleman had been responsible for her brother's murder. But Liza never knew how much she risked until the night she came face-to-face with the dangerously arresting and savagely handsome viscount himself.

_____29576-4 $5.50/$6.50 in Canada

● SINS OF INNOCENCE
by Jean Stone

They were four women with only one thing in common: each gave up her baby to a stranger. They'd met in a home for unwed mothers, where all they had to hold on to was each other. Now, twenty-five years later, it's time to go back and face the past.

_____56342-4 $5.99/$6.99 n Canada

Ask for these books at your local bookstore or use this page to order.

❏ Please send me the books I have checked above. I am enclosing $ _____ (add $2.50 to cover postage and handling). Send check or money order, no cash or C. O. D.'s please.

Name _____

Address _____

City/ State/ Zip _____

Send order to: Bantam Books, Dept. FN134, 2451 S. Wolf Rd., Des Plaines, IL 60018

Allow four to six weeks for delivery.

Prices and availability subject to change without notice.   FN 134 3/94